PUFFIN BOOKS

Published by the Penguin Group: London, New York, Australia, Canada, India,
Ireland, New Zealand and South Africa

Penguin Books Ltd, Registered Offices: 80 Strand, London WC2R 0RL, England

puffinbooks.com

First published 2014

001

Written by Steve Cleverley
Text and illustrations copyright © Mind Candy, 2014
Moshi Monsters is a trademark of Mind Candy Ltd.
All rights reserved

Made and printed in Slovakia

British Library Cataloguing in Publication Data

A CIP catalogue record for this book is
available from the British Library

ISBN: 978–0–141–35276–3

THE ALL-NEW MOSHLINGS COLLECTOR'S GUIDE

PUFFIN

CONTENTS

A MESSAGE FROM BUSTER

Hello, Moshling fans!
Buster Bumblechops at your service.

Unless you've been living in a ditch in the middle of the Gombala Gombala Jungle with your head in a bucket of custard, you should know that I'm the most famous Moshlingologist in the world of Moshi.

Come to think of it, I'm the only Moshlingologist in the world of Moshi. At least I was. You see my assistant Snuffy Hookums has been missing, presumed consumed by a mysterious tribe of unknown Moshlings near the lava lake of Mount KrakkaBlowa. But now she's back!

You could have twisted my gooberries, slapped me silly and called me Sally when she stumbled through the door here at Bumblechops Manor. I thought she was gone for good but it seems she just got a little lost. Silly Snuffy!

Where was I? Oh yes, as I was saying, collecting Moshlings is my business, and business is good. In fact, it's excellent!

6

Just lately, I've been on so many expeditions and discovered so many new Moshlings that I decided to write this fact-packed book to keep track of them all. My goopendous new Moshling Sanctuary will be bursting at the seams!

The following pages are teeming with new discoveries, from Cranky Codfathers to Glamster Hamsters. You'll even get to read about Zoshlings, Moshling-like space critters from beyond the Way-Outta-Sphere!

So sit back, put your paws up, grab a cup of hot gloop soup and prepare to be amazed. Good hunting!

Buster Rumblechops

COLLECTING MOSHLINGS

When it comes to collecting Moshlings, I'm quite the expert. So have a look at my seed-tastic tips. They're sure to grow on you!

MOSHLING SEEDS

As any budding collector knows, Moshlings are attracted to flowers – and seeds make flowers. Just head to the Seed Cart by the Gross-ery Store on Main Street and get shopping. If you're a Moshi Member you can visit The Port area and buy Super Seeds to attract members-only Moshlings!

Next, plant your seeds in your garden and watch them grow. Sounds easy-peasy gooberry-squeezy, eh? Well, sometimes it is but different blooms attract different Moshlings, so be sure to get your combinations just right.

You can also access the Moshling Guide in your garden. Simply select the Moshling you're after and the Guide will tell you which seeds you need. You can even buy and plant the seeds in one go, thus avoiding the hassle of shopping!

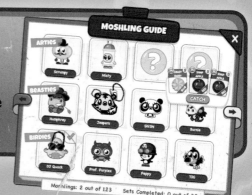

MY GOOPENDOUS MOSHLING SANCTUARY!

It's been the talk of Monstro City for as long as Elder Furi's been growing his beard, but my mind-blowing Moshling Sanctuary is finally taking shape. Prepare to be amazed!

The sanctuary is covered by giant bio-domes, made using huge jelly moulds that date back to the Great Custard Flood of 99999.5. As well as helping to control the climate, these gob-smacking domes keep Moshlings inside and baddies like Dr. Strangeglove out.

Thousands of Roarkers are beavering away to complete parts of the sanctuary. I can reveal that it contains an on-site moshpital, a state-of-the-art hatchery and even a Glump rehabilitation centre!

The sanctuary contains rivers, waterfalls, mountains, deserts, fields and forests. In fact, there's every type of landscape to accommodate all the different Moshlings.

I'm designing a high-tech Moshi monorail to whizz me around the sanctuary's various zones. Mind the gap!

9

ARTIES

I collect art so these paint-slinging Moshlings fascinate me. I recently asked some Abstract Artistes and a few Artful Splodgers to redecorate my Museum of Moshiness after Dr. Strangeglove and his Glumps broke in and vandalized the place. The trouble is it looks even worse now! Oh well. In fact, a Playful Pfft Pfft is spraying a pop-art portrait of me at this very moment. I think it makes me look like a vintage tin of gloop soup!

PAGE 36
Bodge
the Artful Splodger

PAGE 100
Misty
the Playful Pfft Pfft

PAGE 134
Splatter
the Abstract Artiste

BRAINIES

I'm no dummy in the science stakes but Brainies put me in the shade. These super intelligent Moshlings have major brainpower. They even make Elder Furi look dim. Speaking of Elder Furi, he's asked a Joyful Juicy Brainiac to make a de-Glumping device to foil Dr. Strangeglove. And a Molecular Chef is already creating a contraption that freezes baddies in vapour. C.L.O.N.C. won't know what's hit 'em!

PAGE 112
Pinestein
the Joyful Juicy Brainiac

PAGE 120
Prof. Heff
the Molecular Chef

CUTIES

How cute!

PAGE 38
Bubbly
the Rubbery Bubbery

PAGE 44
Chirpy
the Chipper Chaffinch

Awww, I'm just a big softy at heart so I love Cuties. These adorable Moshlings include Rubbery Bubberies and Chipper Chaffinches. But although they look super sweet, Cuties can be pretty tricksy, especially if you try to give one a cuddle. I've been pecked by a Chipper Chaffinch for attempting to stroke it, and almost throttled by a Rubbery Bubbery for squeezing its squishy cheeks. I'll stick to hugging my teddy next time!

FROSTIES

Did you know a Dainty Deer's favourite game is snowflake hoopla? Fun but ffffreezing!

PAGE 164
Willow
the Dainty Deer

Brrr! Despite my thick coat of fur and thermal undies I still feel the cold. And that's bad news for me because Frosties love hanging out in the iciest areas in the world. I built an igloo in the foothills of Mount Sillimanjaro last winter to study Dainty Deers in their natural habitat. But I forgot my mittens and had to dunk my frozzicated fingers in mugs of hot gloop soup to warm up!

FRUITIES

Walking talking fruit? It sounds pretty bonkers but that's the deal with Fruities. I try to meet at least five of these juicy little Moshlings a day because it helps keep me healthy. Let me tell you, working out alongside a Fizzical Phewberry or taking on a Square Pear in a pip-spitting contest is exhausting and always has me reaching for a smoothie. Mmm, fruity!

Fruity business!

PAGE 54
Eugene
the Square Pear

PAGE 114
Pipsi
the Fizzical Phewberry

FUZZIES

I haven't had a fur-cut in ages. But if you think I'm furry now, you should have seen me back in my Moshiversity days. I couldn't walk down Main Street without tripping over my goatee! Perhaps that's why I have a soft spot for Fuzzies. These fleecy Moshlings are pretty varied but they all have one thing in common: they are really fuzzy!

PAGE 122
Quincy
the Fraidy FuzzFace

PAGE 146
Threddie
the Thockity Wock

GIFTIES

Gifties just keep on giving!

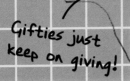

PAGE 106
Nancy
the Flouncy Fancy

They say giving gifts is more satisfying than receiving them, but that's not entirely true when it comes to Gifties. These little Moshlings enjoy giving presents, getting presents and even making presents! And it doesn't need to be a special occasion. I bumped into a gaggle of Gifties at the annual Moshi Garden Fête and they showered me with confetti and plonked a pink rosette on my prize gooberries. How embarrassing!

GURUS

PAGE 68
Hocus
the Wonky Wizard

PAGE 166
Wuzzle
the Wandering Wumple

I've advised many a Moshling over the years. In fact, I see myself as a bit of a guru. But I've never performed a hex in front of royalty like a Wonky Wizard or meditated upside-down like a Wandering Wumple. You see, unlike me, Gurus can be pretty mystical. Now if you'll excuse me I'm off for a lie-down under my enchanted crystals to listen to my new album of ancient Hoodoo chants.

HIPSTERS

I'm not getting any younger but you can bet your flowery flares I'm still 'down' with the youngsters. Hipster Moshlings often nod in approval when they see me dressed up for a night on the town. I'm not quite sure why they giggle and point afterwards though. After all, Jazzy Wigglers, Glamster Hamsters, Swaggering Swines and Creative Coyotes are amongst the coolest Moshlings of all. Surely they're hip to my jive?

PAGE 66
Hissy
the Jazzy Wiggler

PAGE 142
Swizzle
the Swaggering Swine

PAGE 160
Vinnie
the Glamster Hamster

PAGE 170
YoYo
the Creative Coyote

LUCKIES

Do you feel lucky? Well, do you? I do, but that's because I always try to surround myself with Luckies. Unlucky Larrikins are the exception to the rule, of course, and Mystic Moggies are rather unpredictable with their weird magic. But Mini Monies and Kittens of Good Fortune are luckier than a horseshoe-shaped Funny Bunny paw covered in four-leafed clover!

PAGE 60
Furnando
the Mystic Moggy

Mystic Moggies levitate when they meow.

MOVIES

PAGE 32 — **Blinki** the All-Seeing Moment Muncher

PAGE 58 — **Fitch** the Flat-Tailed Fuzzle

PAGE 74 — **Jackson** the Dapper Clapper

PAGE 96 — **Marty** the Mouthy Mogul

Ever since I co-starred in *Moshi Monsters: The Movie*, I've developed a new appreciation for these film-loving Moshlings. Movies make perfect pets for gooperstars because they are impressed by anything to do with the big screen. I might even ask an All-Seeing Moment Muncher to join me on my next expedition. Then I can film everything instead of having to write it down.

MUNCHIES

Is it time for munch yet?

PAGE 148 — **Toasty** the Buttery Breadhead

PAGE 168 — **Yolka** the Boiled Boffin

I'm always getting the Munchies, especially early in the morning. But I'm not talking about a case of the nibbles, I mean these tasty-looking Moshlings. Munchies are at their most active before sunrise, so that's when I go out looking for them. Whether it's brekkie with a Boiled Boffin or elevenses with a Buttery Breadhead, I always enjoy a quick snack whilst observing Munchies. Why? Well, they look good enough to eat!

MUSOS

I'm not much of a musician but I do like parping my kazoo from time to time. Musos love cool music but haven't got time for old 'Bum-note Bumblechops'. Cheek! That said, I did consider putting together a Muso band and entering the M Factor. Thankfully a Boogie-Woogie Bugle and a Punky Monkey talked me out of it after just one rehearsal. They said Simon Growl would split his high pants laughing. Rrrude!

PAGE 72 — **Hot Wings** the Ragamuffin Puffin

PAGE 104 — **Mumbo** the Punky Monkey

PAGE 150 — **Toots** the Boogie-Woogie Bugle

MYTHIES

I've heard millions of myths on my travels but none are as outlandish as the ones surrounding Mythies. This legendary set of Moshlings includes Valiant Vikings and Ginger McMoshlings. But even they can't compete with the tall stories surrounding the Bumblechops family.

My Great Uncle Snufflepeeps once told me that my ancestors were kings of Splatlantis, princes of the swooniverse and owners of a small chain of shoe shops. A likely tale!

PAGE 86 — **Long Beard** the Valiant Viking

NAUGHTIES

PAGE 92
Marcel
Le Uppity Croc Monsieur

PAGE 126
Raffles
the Sneaky TeaLeaf

PAGE 130
Shoney
the Amazin' Blazin' Raisin

PAGE 162
Weeny
the Teeny Genie

These mischievous Moshlings are always causing trouble. On a recent fact-finding trip to a Naughties convention I had my socks stolen by a Sneaky TeaLeaf, my backside toasted by an Amazin' Blazin' Raisin, and my face covered in enchanted bubblegum thanks to a Teeny Genie. To cap it all, an Uppity Croc Monsieur bit me when I complained!

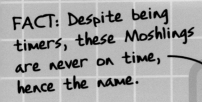

FACT: Despite being timers, these Moshlings are never on time, hence the name.

NICK NACKS

Before I met this mingle-mangle of Moshlings I thought Nick Nacks were objects that collected dust on the mantelpiece. But I

PAGE 152
Topsy Turvy
the Tardy Timer

PAGE 27
Peeps
the Bowtied Bookling

realize now they are more than just tourist mementos. In fact, I'm going on a mini expedition very soon to search the lofts, cellars and drawers of Monstro City, as I hear Nick Nacks love to hide in such places. I might even look in the boot of my Bumble Buggy because that's where I discovered my first Tardy Timer!

NUTTIES

Caution: this set may contain nuts. Well, not quite, but the Nutties are certainly tough nuts to crack because their protective shells are rock hard. But once you get to know them they are a friendly bunch. I've encountered Nutties all over the world of Moshi, from Goober Gulch and the Gombala Gombala Jungle to Wingledeed Woods. I even presented a live gardening show alongside a Woodland Walnut in Wobbly Woods!

PAGE 108
Nutmeg
the Woodland Walnut

Woodland Walnuts are totally crazy about nature.

POTTIES

You'd think being stuck in a pot might be a bit annoying, but Potties seem to love it. I do too, as it makes collecting these cute little critters easier than pulling your socks up. I even allow a few Potties inside Bumblechops Manor. They're fang-tastic houseguests but you have to be careful – sitting on a snoozing Tickly Pickle is a real pain in the backside. Spiky!

PAGE 34
Blossom
the Blooming Wonder

PAGE 118
Prickles
The Tickly Pickle

PUZZLIES

The real puzzle about Puzzlies is how these head-scratchingly strange Moshlings remained hidden for so long! They really are riddles wrapped in enigmas inside a moshtery. Or funny-looking critters, depending on your point of view! I'm thinking of installing a games room in Bumblechops Manor so that all the Puzzlies I've collected can play together. I'd love to know if a Baffled Bit could beat a Nifty Shifty in a game of Mosh/Mash!

PAGE 80 — **Jiggy** the Baffled Bit

PAGE 154 — **Tumbles** the Nifty Shifty

ROXSTARS

The Daily Growl once described me as the 'original rock star of Moshlingology'. That's very flattering, but I'm not a true Roxstar. Creepy Crooners and Quirky Koalas are flamboyant little Moshlings who love performing in public. Well they like showing off in restaurants and posing on Stardust Street! The nearest I've come to anything that showy is fronting the TV ad campaign for Wobble-ade. It's the fizziest dizziest soda in town, don't you know!

PAGE 70 — **Hoolio** the Creepy Crooner

PAGE 172 — **Ziggy** the Quirky Koala

SALTIES

I've just put a huge aquarium in my Moshling Sanctuary for all the Salties I've discovered. Sometimes I slip on my flippers and dive in to watch their watery ways. It's great fun bobbing along with Mollycoddled Manamanas, but Selfish Shellfish are a different story, as they enjoy nipping my toes, biting my nose and shoving their magical pearls down my snorkel.

PAGE 84
Linton
the Mollycoddled Manamana

PAGE 128
Shimmy
the Selfish Shellfish

SCREAMIES

When you've been on as many adventures as me, fear is not an option. But even I felt a shiver down my spine the first time I saw the Screamies. Probably because a Boggy Swampling had just plopped an ice cube down my back! But I've grown to love these creepy Moshlings. Apart from Little Red Riding Wolves, their bark is usually worse than their bite. I even took a Gone-Wrong Blob to a Halloween bash at Goosebump Manor. Unfortunately the poor thing was mistaken for a jelly and covered in custard!

PAGE 62
Glob
the Gone-Wrong Blob

PAGE 76
Jibbly
the Dearly-Departed Nibbly

PAGE 94
Marsha
the Boggy Swampling

PAGE 124
Randall
the Little Red Riding Wolf

SECRETS

Psst, wanna know a secret? These very special Moshlings include Baby Rox, the controversial Glitzy BooHoo, who replaced the artist formerly known as . . . no, I can't tell you, it's a secret. All I can say is that she threw her toys out of the pram before vanishing! And if you think that's weird, wait until you hear about the other Secrets, highly collectable critters that . . . oops, sorry, time for me to zip it!

PAGE 28
Baby Rox
the Glitzy BooHoo

Sweet talkin, smiling and beguiling.

SMILIES

Some say a smile's just a curve that sets everything straight. But if that were true I wouldn't have got into such a pickle for smiling at a Smiley Moshling. It wasn't a Sparkly Sweetheart or even a Jabbering Jibberling. A Persuasive Pusskins mesmerized me into giving it all my supplies before vanishing into Wobbly Woods. It even took my socks!

PAGE 64
Grinny
the Persuasive Pusskins

SPARKLIES

A sprinkle of magic is sometimes all you need to solve a tricky situation. But Luvli can't be on hand 24/7, so that's when I turn to the Sparklies. These enchanting Moshlings have special powers. Forgetful Fairies can sew daisy chains together – perfect for rescuing Moshlingologists who've tumbled into custard swamps. And Shooting Stars can travel faster than the speed of light so they can save you before you've even fallen in!

PAGE 116
Posy
the Forgetful Fairy

PAGE 144
Tessa
the Shooting Star

Add a touch of sparkle to your life.

SPLOSHIES

Whenever I set sail on Potion Ocean aboard my research ship, the *Windigo II*, I always take a few Sploshies along because these soggy Moshlings make ideal crewmates. I use a Supah Loofah to swab the deck, a Splodgy Sucker to plug any leaks, a Cranky Codfather to help navigate stormy seas, and a Magical Tinkler to spread joy and happiness amongst the crew. Yo, ho, ho!

PAGE 30
Bentley
the Supah Loofah

PAGE 138
Sprinkles
the Magical Tinkler

PAGE 140
Sweeney Blob
the Splodgy Sucker

PAGE 158
Uncle Scallops
the Cranky Codfather

SPORTIES

Forget Trembly Stadium, here within my Moshling Sanctuary I'm building a giant enormodome so that all my Sporties can compete in the all-new Moshlympics. Several Boinging Balls are organizing a boinging tournament, and a team of Humongous Hogsnorters are flexing their pecs outside as I write. But they're not competing, they're helping to lay the Astroturf!

PAGE 52   **Dribbles** the Boinging Ball

PAGE 88   **Lummox** the Humongous Hogsnorter

TECHIES 2.0

PAGE 48   **Cosmo** the Mini Moshulator

PAGE 98   **Micro Dave** the Popty-Ping

PAGE 78   **Jiggles** the Fiddly TwiddleStick

I can't get my head around all these newfangled gadgets. I even toasted my ear with the iron when my new phone rang the other day! Thankfully, Techies 2.0 are user-friendly Moshlings. I've cooked supper with a Popty-Ping, calculated the cost of my whaccurrants using a Mini Moshulator and had a quick wiggle on a Fiddly TwiddleStick. They really are clever little gizmos but . . . sorry, must dash, I need to shovel coal into my computer.

TOOMIES

Exploring ancient temples is one of my favourite hobbies so I often head to the banks of the River Smile or the Yakkety Sax Sandbar in search of new Moshlings. Getting sand in your socks is annoying but it's worth it to hang out with Toomies. Just the other day I performed a moonlit sand dance with a Barking RahRah and had a go on a Funky Pharaoh's ancient golden saxophone.

Toot-tastic!

PAGE 42
Carter
the Barking RahRah

PAGE 82
King Toot
the Funky Pharaoh

WHEELIES

I love anything with wheels, and often spend hours whizzing around in my Bumble Buggy. But even my driving skills can't compete with Wheelies. These nippy critters are tricky to track as they can zoom round all kinds of terrain at breakneck speeds. That's why I usually try to herd them towards the nearest flight of stairs because Wheelies struggle with steps – and so do I when I forget I'm wearing my roller skates. Aaargh!

PAGE 174
Zonkers
the Bonkers Whizzling

WOODIES

Timberrr! Sometimes you can't see the Woodies for the trees – and that's because these forest-dwelling Moshlings aren't keen to meet Moshlingologists. Oakey-Dokey Hokey-Pokies, for instance, are usually too busy hiding in bushes to come and play. But who can blame them when villains such as Biggie Diddles III rip down Moshi forests in search of buried custard and hidden chocolate? It's my new eco mission to stop him!

PAGE 110

Peekaboo
the Oakey-Dokey Hokey-Pokey

YEEHAWS

The only seal afraid of water!

Tickle my pickle and slap my silly sausages! Sorry, but I can't help talking in an excitable manner whenever I come across a Yeehaw. These hick-tastic Moshlings are often misunderstood because they spend so much time line-dancing around Whoop 'n' Holler Valley. I find talking to them in a slow drawl whilst chewing shredded Oobla Doobla gets the best response. The last time I spoke to a Seal with a Reel in my normal voice he took offence and hit me with a hubcap.

PAGE 46

Cleetus
the Seal with a Reel

YUCKIES

I've done some pretty yucky things on expeditions over the years. But swimming in curdled custard and having a Pixel-Munching Snaffler barf a rainbow on your shoes doesn't compare to the Yuckies. This icky Moshling set includes Lickity Lizards and Sniffly Splurgees. And let's not even mention Waddling Floffles because the last time I saw one it spewed a tummy-full of barbecued ladybird wings over my head. And I wasn't wearing my hat. :(

PAGE 90
Lurgee
the Sniffly Splurgee

PAGE 132
Slurpy
the Lickity Lizard

PAGE 156
Twaddle
the Waddling Floffle

ZOSHLINGS

I'd heard rumours of Zoshling sightings for many moons. But it wasn't until the Zoshlings' *Rhapsody 2* spaceship crashlanded on Music Island that I became a true believer. Since then I've had several close encounters of the Zoshi kind. I've even ridden on Splutnik's jetpack and sampled some of First Officer Ooze's cosmic gloop. It's out of this world!

PAGE 40
Captain Squirk

PAGE 50
Dr. C. Fingz

PAGE 56
First Officer Ooze

PAGE 136
Splutnik

PEEPS
THE BOWTIED BOOKLING

Personality:
- ✓ Bookish
- ✓ Geeky
- ✓ Wordy

HABITAT
Most Bowtied Booklings enjoy the silence of libraries but you might find a few shushing each other from the shelves of Biblio Boulevard.

CODE TO CATCH PEEPS:
EXCLUSIVE
with this book, The All-New Moshling Collector's Guide.

Shhh! Fingers on lips and listen up because Bowtied Booklings can recite every Moshi story ever written. Just pull on that elasticated bow tie, whisper the title of your favourite tale and presto! These well-read Moshlings can even spell out any Moshi word, including 'gooperdoopermoshdabbytastic'.

Don't turn the page on this well-read wordsmith without finding out how to add one to your collection! Send me an email at **busterbumblechops@ moshimonsters.com** and I'll reveal the secret!

LIKES Swallowing dictionaries and saying 'shhhh'

DISLIKES E-readers and Owls of Wiseness

RARE

BABY ROX
THE GLITZY BOOHOO

Personality:
- ☑ Diva-ish
- ☑ Babyish
- ☑ Outlandish

 LIKES Mashed blurghnips and moonwalking on talcum powder

 DISLIKES Bedtime and baby talk

TO CATCH BABY ROX:
Complete **SEASON 1**, **MISSION 1** of the Super Moshi Missions.

Some gooperstars like throwing their toys out of the pram. But not Baby Rox. I've yet to hear her toe-tapping music but the monsters at HighPants Productions tell me that this wah-wah-ing Moshling is all set to take Monstro City by storm! I spoke to her high-trousered manager Simon Growl recently and he told me that this blinged-up baby enjoys dunking rusks in milky-wilk, rocking the cradle with her techno lullabies and bustin' out cutesy moves. (If any of you know what 'techno' is, I'm all ears!)

HABITAT

Like most Glitzy BooHoos, Baby Rox was born in Nappy Valley. These days you'll find her boo-hoo-ing in Diddums Dale.

Ultra rare!

BENTLEY
THE SUPAH LOOFAH

CODE TO CATCH BENTLEY:

STAR BLOSSOM — BLACK + STAR BLOSSOM — BLACK + MOON ORCHID — BLACK

I read that Supah Loofahs were once used as back-scrubbers by rich monsters, so I thought I'd give one a try. It was quite delightful as I'd been trying to get a Tickly Pickle's itching powder off my back all week. Apart from their soothing qualities, Supah Loofahs are helpful little Moshlings who can hold half an ocean's worth of water in their squishy bodies. And that's just as well 'cos if they stay in the sun for too long they dry out and crumble to bits. That's why it's always good to have a Magical Tinkler on hand if you decide to go looking for Supah Loofahs during a heatwave.

LIKES

Power showers and being squished

DISLIKES

Bubble bath and flaky skin

HABITAT

You'll always find them in the bathroom at parties but they love soaking up the atmosphere (and water) in Reggae Reef.

Ultra rare!

31

BLINKI
THE ALL-SEEING MOMENT MUNCHER

Personality:
- ☑ Inquisitive
- ☑ Kind
- ☑ Brave

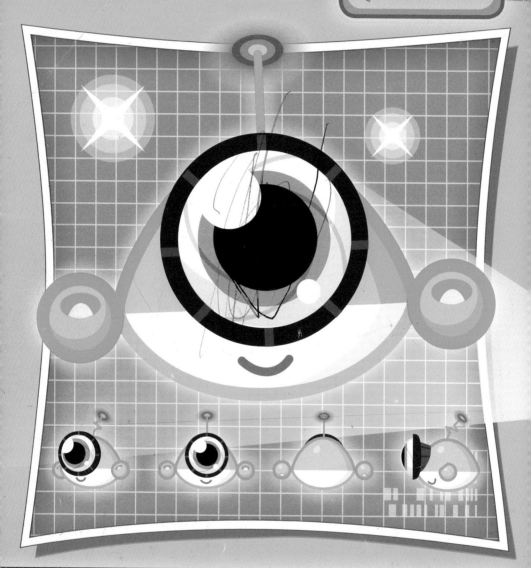

LIKES
Lens wipes and adventure stories

DISLIKES
Hot Hoodoo stew and kerfuffling

CODE TO CATCH BLINKI:
Head to the **GOMBALA GOMBALA JUNGLE** and complete the **BUG RUSH MINI GAME.**

My good friend Roary Scrawl knows much more about these fascinating Moshlings than I do. But that's hardly surprising because Roary uses one called Blinki to make movies. With their long-range Moshiscopic lenses, nifty side-jets and twiddly transmitters, All-Seeing Moment Munchers are fully equipped to capture any event. And that's just as well because they can also play back the moments they munch via their built-in holographic projectors. I might take one on my next expedition, but only if it promises not to follow me when I'm changing. Well, I don't want the whole world knowing about my Zack Binspin underpants . . .

OOPS!

HABITAT

Wherever Roary Scrawl goes Blinki follows, but it is believed this all-seeing sidekick first popped up on Shutter Island.

Ultra rare!

BLOSSOM
THE BLOOMING WONDER

Personality:
- ☑ Optimistic
- ☑ Humble
- ☑ Welcoming

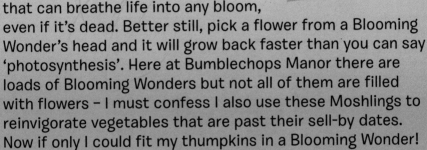

Do you love flowers as much as I do? Well, next time they look sad try popping them in a Blooming Wonder. These miraculous Moshlings are infused with enchanted fertilizer that can breathe life into any bloom, even if it's dead. Better still, pick a flower from a Blooming Wonder's head and it will grow back faster than you can say 'photosynthesis'. Here at Bumblechops Manor there are loads of Blooming Wonders but not all of them are filled with flowers – I must confess I also use these Moshlings to reinvigorate vegetables that are past their sell-by dates. Now if only I could fit my thumpkins in a Blooming Wonder!

HABITAT

You'll usually find Blooming Wonders promenading in Petal Park or sitting on windowsills across Monstro City.

LIKES Slug pellets and sunshine

DISLIKES Dirty water and thieving bees

CODE TO CATCH BLOSSOM:

DRAGON FRUIT
ANY

+

MAGIC BEANS
ANY

+

CRAZY DAISY
ANY

COMMON

BODGE
THE ARTFUL SPLODGER

Personality:
- ☑ Scatterbrained
- ☑ Screwy
- ☑ Sloppy

CODE TO CATCH BODGE:

HOT SILLY PEPPERS ANY + DRAGON FRUIT ANY + LOVE BERRIES ANY

Why do a job properly when you can bodge it? Why indeed, because Artful Splodgers are the messy Moshlings who just love slopping paint all over the place. I made the mistake of hiring a team of Artful Splodgers to redecorate my bedroom here at Bumblechops Manor. What a disaster! I've still got paint on my paws and the ceiling looks as if I.G.G.Y. has thrown up one of his colourful rainbows all over it! When they are not messing up Moshi houses these playful paint pots enjoy creating foot paintings of famous monsters. In fact, they offered to do one of me but I politely declined. Look out, wet paint!

HABITAT

Peek in any cellar and you might find an Artful Splodger chilling out next to an old bag of cement. Failing that, head to the Googenheim.

GOOGENHEIM ART GALLERY

OPEN

LIKES

Licking sandpaper and blank walls

DISLIKES

Stiff paintbrushes and wallpaper

COMMON

37

BUBBLY
THE RUBBERY BUBBERY

Personality:
- ☑ Flexible
- ☑ Emotional
- ☑ Vivacious

CODE TO CATCH BUBBLY:

CRAZY DAISY ANY + CRAZY DAISY ANY + CRAZY DAISY ANY

Squishy beyond belief, Rubbery Bubberies are the stretchiest Moshlings ever. If my calculations are correct I believe these gentle, jelly-headed creatures can stretch their tentacles around the entire world of Moshi three times over and still reach the top shelf in the Gross-ery Store. I might test this theory out one day, as I love getting my name in *The Moshi Book of Records*. The only problem is that Rubbery Bubberies are goopendously slippery. And I should know because the last time I tried to pull one out from under a rock it boinged in my face like a big sloppy rubber band.

OUCH!

LIKES Purple sprouting seaweed and Batty Bubblefish

DISLIKES Pebbly beaches and the sound of balloons being rubbed

HABITAT

Set sail on Potion Ocean and you'll probably see a few Rubbery Bubberies bobbing about on the foamy waves.

COMMON

CAPTAIN SQUIRK

Personality:
- ✓ Heroic
- ✓ Bold
- ✓ Trailblazing

LIKES

Planet-hopping and squirmholes

DISLIKES

Violin bows and turbulence

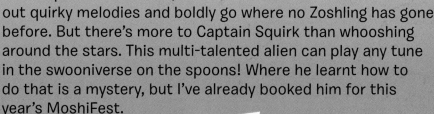

I'm a Moshlingologist, not a Zoshlingolist, so all I can do is explain what Tamara Tesla told me about this strange little chap. As brave captain of the *Rhapsody 2*, Squirk's mission is to explore new worlds, seek out quirky melodies and boldly go where no Zoshling has gone before. But there's more to Captain Squirk than whooshing around the stars. This multi-talented alien can play any tune in the swooniverse on the spoons! Where he learnt how to do that is a mystery, but I've already booked him for this year's MoshiFest.

HABITAT

The planet Symphonia but Squirk can often be found traversing the Swooniverse aboard the *Rhapsody 2*.

TO CATCH CAPTAIN SQUIRK: Complete **SEASON 2, MISSION 10** of the Super Moshi Missions.

Ultra rare!

CARTER
THE BARKING RAHRAH

Personality:
- ☑ Crackers
- ☑ Loyal
- ☑ Dippy

Only mad dogs and Barking RahRahs go out in the midday sun. Well, that's what I hear, and perhaps it explains why these sun-worshipping Moshlings enjoy shuffle-dancing in the sand and striking weird poses from ancient tomb paintings. But is a Barking RahRah's bark worse than its bite? You bet, because whenever they attack they sound like Silly Snufflers sitting on broken kazoos. Having said that, whenever I visit the Lost Valley of iSissi I just can't resist joining in with their daft dancing. Believe me, getting sand kicked in your face has never been such fun!

 LIKES Kicking sand and being fanned

 DISLIKES Cheap jewellery and floppy ears

HABITAT

Barking RahRahs live amongst the ancient ruins of Old Geeza near the Lost Valley of iSissi.

 Ultra rare!

CHIRPY
THE CHIPPER CHAFFINCH

Personality:
- ☑ Optimistic
- ☑ Jaunty
- ☑ Cute

TO CATCH CHIRPY:

MOON ORCHID PINK + MOON ORCHID PINK + CRAZY DAISY ANY

Knock knock! Who's there? No, it's not a Perky Pecker, it's a Chipper Chaffinch. It's an easy mistake because these impossibly cute Moshlings are always pecking away at trees, tip-tapping messages to each other in Mosh Code. Things like 'peckity . . . peck . . . thud', which, roughly translated, means 'I love you, too'. Whenever I'm camping in Wobbly Woods I try to whistle a few jolly tunes for the local Chipper Chaffinches (I'm pretty good, if I do say so myself) because they can't whistle. But I think they prefer the knockity-knock sound of me bashing tent pegs with my mallet, although they do sometimes flutter past and give me a peck on the cheek. Ooh, it tickles!

LIKES Flying south and knocking on wood

DISLIKES Jet engines and eleven secret herbs and spices

HABITAT

In brightly painted bird boxes, high up in the trees of Wobbly Woods.

RARE

CLEETUS
THE SEAL WITH A REEL

Personality:
- ☑ Simple
- ☑ Deluded
- ☑ Talkative

 LIKES Chewing fishpaste and conspiracy theories

 DISLIKES Navy Seals and fancy pants

TO CATCH CLEETUS:

LOVE BERRIES ANY + LOVE BERRIES ANY + SNAP APPLE ANY

If you're looking for a Seal with a Reel don't bother heading to Potion Ocean, or even Croak Creek, because these fishing-crazy Moshlings are afraid of water. I spent ages sailing the Seventy Seas in search of just one of these slippery fellas and where do you think I eventually found one? Yep, you guessed it, in a fishing tackle shop near Stinky Hollow. So what's with the reel? Well, Seals with Reels just love hooking rusty hubcaps onto their fishing lines and pretending they are flying saucers.

HABITAT

You will usually find a few Seals with Reels barking on the rocks of the dried-up riverbed running through Whoop 'n' Holler Valley.

COMMON

COSMO
THE MINI MOSHULATOR

Personality:
- ☑ Logical
- ☑ Bright
- ☑ Thoughtful

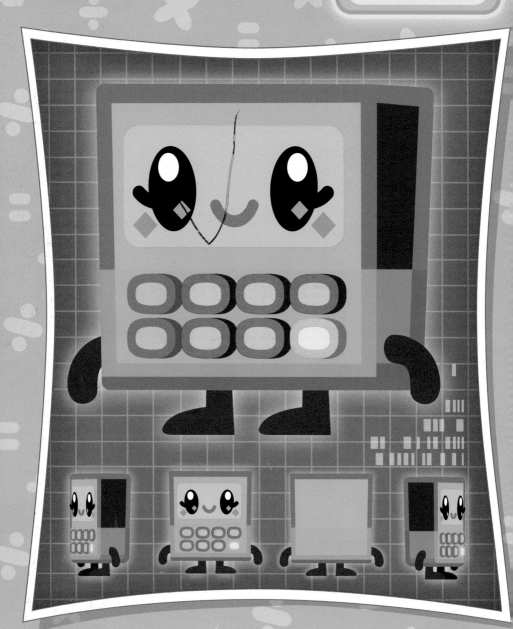

Despite being a master Moshlingologist, my maths is pretty awful. That's why I keep a Mini Moshulator in my bag. Able to calculate the cost of a billion gooberries in seconds, these friendly Moshlings can be counted on in any situation – literally because they love having their buttons pushed. Press 'em in a certain order and they may even hand you a printout of a popular equation and beep a fraction of a tune. But never put one near a Mini Moshifone because, thanks to a new app, Moshifones are now better at sums!

$= 86$ 52

$\sqrt{ZX \sim M \times 2}$

$f(x) = \dfrac{X}{3} + 5$

$\displaystyle\int_3^1 \dfrac{4z}{2\pi}$ $\cos\left(\dfrac{2010.2}{7}\right) = CHEESE$

TO CATCH COSMO:

HOT SILLY PEPPERS **BLACK** + HOT SILLY PEPPERS **BLACK** + HOT SILLY PEPPERS **BLACK**

HABITAT

Often seen with Tabby Nerdicats near Honeycomb Hill, Mini Moshulators love hiding in drawers.

Ultra rare!

LIKES Long division and exams

DISLIKES Sausage fingers and cheapo batteries

DR. C. FINGZ

Personality:
- ✓ Perceptive
- ✓ Professorial
- ✓ Quirky

 LIKES Messy handwriting and powdered egg

 DISLIKES Clowns and top hats

Dr. C. Fingz's sick bay

Able to read minds via his telepathic wiggle-stalk, Dr. C. Fingz is the *Rhapsody 2*'s chief medical officer. I could have done with his help that time I was smacked in the gooberries by a Valiant Viking's rubber hammer. Ouch! When he's not bandaging up battered Zoshlings, this fuzzy fella uses his powers to communicate with alien beings across the swooniverse. The good doctor can even temporarily extract talent from other critters, so one minute he can move like Bobbi SingSong, the next he can sing like Zack Binspin. I do hope he never meets Strangeglove – the results could be disastrous!

TO CATCH DR. C. FINGZ:

Complete **SEASON 2, MISSION 10** of the Super Moshi Missions.

Ultra rare!

HABITAT

The planet Symphonia but Dr. C. Fingz has also made guest appearances at the circus on Music Island.

DRIBBLES
THE BOINGING BALL

Personality:
- ☑ Competitive
- ☑ Sporty
- ☑ Lively

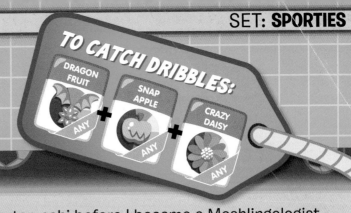

TO CATCH DRIBBLES:

DRAGON FRUIT
ANY
+
SNAP APPLE
ANY
+
CRAZY DAISY
ANY

I was a keen sportsmoshi before I became a Moshlingologist. In fact, I could have turned pro if I hadn't hurt my back playing marbles. Perhaps that's why I always enjoy a good kick about with a few Boinging Balls. These round little Moshlings love it, especially if it involves being booted into the back of a net. Goooal! They also enjoy getting stuck up trees and leaping into their neighbours' gardens.

Famed for their incredible bouncability and competitive streak, Boinging Balls take deep breaths to avoid feeling deflated, and will go in goal if you ask nicely. **BOING!**

HABITAT

Boinging Balls often end up in the wrong garden, so if you find one in yours, kick it back to Trembly Stadium.

LIKES
Rolling around in mud and big silvery cups

DISLIKES
Penalty shoot-outs and red cards

COMMON

EUGENE
THE SQUARE PEAR

TO CATCH EUGENE:

HOT SILLY PEPPERS — BLUE + HOT SILLY PEPPERS — ANY + SNAP APPLE — ANY

I'm often accused of being a fuddy-duddy but you'd be surprised how wild I can be. Why, just last night I stayed up until midnight after putting a few drops of Bongo Colada in my cocoa. And I once went to bed without brushing my teeth! But what about Square Pears? Well, the clue is in the name because despite looking fun and fruity, Square Pears are incredibly, er, square. Why? On top of always worrying about what the neighbours will think, these clever but cautious Moshlings are forever tut-tutting about something, whether it's the latest Missy Kix video or the price of Snail Ale.

HABITAT

The rolling orchards of Fuddy-Duddy Farm.

LIKES Putting sticks in the mud and twitching curtains

DISLIKES Pop music and Bongo Colada

UNCOMMON

FIRST OFFICER OOZE

LIKES Gardening and shelling peas

DISLIKES Salt and slug pellets

TO CATCH FIRST OFFICER OOZE:
Complete **SEASON 2, MISSION 10** of the Super Moshi Missions.

Second in command aboard the *Rhapsody 2*, First Officer Ooze is always in demand thanks to all the cosmic gloop he generates. Tamara Tesla tells me that besides oiling all kinds of alien contraptions, this icky stuff has magical auto-tuning properties – a teaspoon a day and you'll be singing like Missy Kix (not that I know much about her!) in no time. It even makes things grow, so I must get some for my beard and Moshling seeds!

HABITAT

The planet Symphonia but Ooze loves growing stuff, so look in the nearest greenhouse.

Ultra rare!

FITCH
THE FLAT-TAILED FUZZLE

Personality:
- ☑ Eager
- ☑ Energetic
- ☑ Ambitious

TO CATCH FITCH:
Complete the **MOSHI MOVIE MYSTERY, PART 4.**

If you're in the movie business you're bound to know a few Flat-Tailed Fuzzles. Ever since I became an accidental movie star thanks to *Moshi Monsters: The Movie*, I've befriended quite a few of these eager beaver-like critters. Renowned for their ability to fetch absolutely anything you desire, 24/7, these perky little Moshlings make ideal gofers. What's more, their sturdy tails are perfect for balancing cups of coffee, fat contracts and egg and cress sandwiches. I'm even thinking of employing a few myself as they are great at running errands around my Moshling Sanctuary. And fetching my tea!

HABITAT

The riverbanks near Three Bags Full Field, but most Flat-Tailed Fuzzles live and work on Moshi movie sets.

LIKES — Blockbusters and golf carts

DISLIKES — Arrogant gooperstars and slowcoaches

RARE

59

FURNANDO
THE MYSTIC MOGGY

Personality:
- ☑ Eccentric
- ☑ Captivating
- ☑ Confident

TO CATCH FURNANDO:
Play the **MOSHLING THEME PARK DS GAME.**

You're feeling sleepy, very sleepy. Well, you will be if you gaze into a Mystic Moggy's eyes. In fact, you might start woofing or oinking because these mysterious Moshlings are talented sorcerers. I found this out when I tried to take a photo of one in the Moshling Theme Park, only to wake up the next day covered in straw and mud. The monster who runs the dodgems in the park told me that Mystic Moggies can even levitate when they meow, cough up magic furballs and make pilchards vanish ('cos they sneak them under their top hats).

GEE WHISKERS!

HABITAT

The Moshling Theme Park. Mystic Moggies have also been spotted selling miracle fur tonic on the outskirts of Main Street.

LIKES

Poker and trick dice

DISLIKES

Hidden cameras and silk hankies

Ultra rare!

GLOB
THE GONE-WRONG BLOB

Personality:
- ☑ Super-brainy
- ☑ Frustrated
- ☑ Eccentric

LIKES
Sub-molecular Moshiology and flower pressing

DISLIKES
Discarded chewing gum and stairs

TO CATCH GLOB:
Complete **MOSHIS VS GHOSTS, HOUSE 1.**

The result of a series of failed experiments, Gone-Wrong Blobs are the squishy squashy Moshlings in search of a cure. These well-meaning dollops were once professors whose attempts to create a mega Moshling went horribly wrong due to a spelling mistake in a teleporter instruction book. I knew a Gone-Wrong Blob when it was still a normal monster. Perhaps that explains why these peculiar Moshlings often gather at the gates of Bumblechops Manor expecting an invite to tea. I sometimes oblige but they always make a mess on my carpets. If I knew anything about particle mutation I could help but all my books on the subject have been gobbled up by – yep, you guessed it – Gone-Wrong Blobs!

HABITAT

You often see these shapeless Moshlings squishing around Tamara Tesla's lab, but many Gone-Wrong Blobs flock to the tunnels beneath the Moshi Fun Park.

COMMON

GRINNY
THE PERSUASIVE PUSSKINS

Personality:
- ☑ Devious
- ☑ Beguiling
- ☑ Smarmy

TO CATCH GRINNY:
Complete **THE BEANSTALK,
PART 2.**

With their amazing powers of persuasion, these catty little Moshlings can sweet-talk you into doing almost anything, even against your will. Not that they could ever fool a wily old fox like me, oh no. In fact, I'm staring into the eyes of a Persuasive Pusskins right now and all it has managed to persuade me to do this morning is fetch it a saucer of chocolate milk, stroke its tummy, bring it fifteen tins of swoonafish on a silver tray, dangle a ball of wool over its head and . . . hang on a second, I've been duped by a Persuasive Pusskins! Well, I never! It's no wonder experts say they can mesmerize monsters with just the slightest grin.

MEOW!

ZZZZZZZZ

HABITAT

Go to Wobbly Woods and you'll probably see a Persuasive Pusskins snoozing high up on a branch.

LIKES
Sipping milk through bendy straws and second-hand car showrooms

DISLIKES
Undercover YapYaps and balls of wool

COMMON

HISSY
THE JAZZY WIGGLER

Personality:
- ✓ Cool
- ✓ Snazzy
- ✓ Slithery

 LIKES Clarinet solos and berets

DISLIKES Squares and stairs

Psst . . . no, it's not a secret, it's the noise Jazzy Wigglers make whenever they hear a wild tune. Not that I make a habit of listening to these hip Moshlings as I don't visit the same clubs as them. In fact, the only club I go to is the Fusty Moshlingologist Country Club, where I sometimes compare etchings with fellow Moshling lovers. Now where was I? Oh yes, as distant relatives of Beatnik Boas, Jazzy Wigglers can't resist making jazzy sounds by poking out their tongues and shaking their jellybean tail rattles. Put simply, they don't wanna hiss a thing! (By the way, their jellybean rattles make great maracas.)

HABITAT

Often seen slithering out of the Purple Banana Jazz Club, Jazzy Wigglers originate from Thelonious Thicket.

TO CATCH HISSY:

HOT SILLY PEPPERS
ANY

+

MOON ORCHID
PURPLE

+

SNAP APPLE
BLACK

RARE

HOCUS
THE WONKY WIZARD

Personality:
- ☑ Forgetful
- ☑ Wise
- ☑ Wonky

TO CATCH HOCUS:

HOT SILLY PEPPERS ANY + **SNAP APPLE** ANY + **SNAP APPLE** ANY

According to a dusty old book I found in the library here at Bumblechops Manor, these scatter-brained sorcerers once entertained Moshi royalty with jaw-dropping feats of magic. But then, one fateful day, a jealous witch made their hats all wonky, causing them to forget their spells. Thankfully Wonky Wizards can still perform using their enchanted curled-up wands, but only on days beginning with Z. I once went to a fancy dress party dressed as a Wonky Wizard but a real one took offence and tried to turn me into a Froggie Doggie.

RIBBIT!

HABITAT

Originally from the mystical land of Alakazam, Wonky Wizards later settled in Presto Place.

LIKES Dungeons and dragons

DISLIKES Square tables and newfangled technology

COMMON

HOOLIO
THE CREEPY CROONER

Personality:
- ☑ Gloomy
- ☑ Tuneless
- ☑ Mysterious

TO CATCH HOOLIO:
Explore Goosebump Manor and complete the **ECTOGLOOP MINI-GAME.**

I see dead Moshlings! Well, not quite, but you could be forgiven for thinking that these eerie Moshlings are dearly departed as they do look pretty lifeless. Then again, Creepy Crooners are dead good on the guitar. These wandering minstrels love playing mournful mariachi music, especially when there is a full moon. With their colourful make-up and snazzy outfits they can often be found in posh Moshi restaurants serenading diners, handing out dead roses and collecting tips in their hats. I must be sure to book one next time I go on a date – which is unlikely as I'm married to Moshlingology!

LIKES Piñatas filled with bugs and rotten tortillas

DISLIKES Daylight and decent melodies

HABITAT

Head to Dearly Departed Drive and you're sure to find a few Creepy Crooners de-tuning their guitars.

UNCOMMON

HOT WINGS
THE RAGAMUFFIN PUFFIN

Personality:
- ☑ Easy-going
- ☑ Philosophical
- ☑ Chilled

TO CATCH HOT WINGS:

DRAGON FRUIT **BLACK** + MOON ORCHID **ANY** + MOON ORCHID **ANY**

Just like me, Ragamuffin Puffins never get in a flap. But that's not because they're super chilled out, it's because they can't fly. Not to worry though, these upbeat Moshlings are usually too busy squawking cheerful songs and performing their signature Rub-A-Dub dance moves to think about going anywhere. I was first introduced to a Ragamuffin Puffin by a group of Disco Duckies at the annual Big Birdie Bash on the Taki Taki Islands. Apparently the beaky little critter was doing some beatboxing on the Orange Sauce Stage but he was on way after my bedtime. Not that it mattered because I could hear the squawking from my tent, even with a pillow over my head.

RESPECT!

HABITAT

Stroll along Dropbeat Drive and you might spot a few Ragamuffin Puffins jammin' to the riddim of DJ Quack's roots remix.

👍 **LIKES**
Rice and peas

👎 **DISLIKES**
Hustle and hard rock

UNCOMMON

JACKSON
THE DAPPER CLAPPER

Personality:
- ☑ Keen
- ☑ Cheerful
- ☑ Diligent

TO CATCH JACKSON:

Head to the Gombala Gombala Jungle and complete **MISSION 3**.

The last time I was exploring near Clackity Cove I felt sure I could hear the unmistakable clack of a Dapper Clapper's snapper. Or perhaps it was just a few sticky crickets singing in the trees. Whatever it was I couldn't investigate further as a Flat-Tailed Fuzzle shooed me away, muttering something about a 'closed set'. You see, Dapper Clappers are movie-loving Moshlings that spend most days hoping to hear 'Action!' or 'Cut!' because these are the only two words that will activate their clickity-clackity heads. Perhaps that's why they are always hanging out with Mouthy Moguls on film sets. If you see one, watch your fingers!

HABITAT

Dapper Clappers sometimes hang around the Moshi TV Studios but I'm convinced they come from Clackity Cove.

LIKES Black and white movies and subtitles

DISLIKES Z-list celebs and trapped fingers

COMMON

75

JIBBLY
THE DEARLY-DEPARTED NIBBLY

Personality:
- ✓ Suave
- ✓ Shambling
- ✓ Skew-whiff

LIKES Fresh meat and funky finger-clicking

DISLIKES Hippies and sledgehammers

TO CATCH JIBBLY:
Head to Goosebump Manor and blast the ghosts in **HOUSE 4**.

Even when I was stranded and starving in the Gombala Gombala jungle, I fought the urge to eat Moshlings. They're just too adorable. And yet, despite being sophisticated high-rollers, Dearly-Departed Nibblies can't resist snacking on their fellow Moshlings. Luckily they only get peckish at night, so they can enjoy spending their days drooling over the finer things in life, such as vintage Wobble-ade, swing music and rancid eyeball roulette. I find the best way to distract a Dearly-Departed Nibbly from chewing a hapless Moshling is to wallop it over the head with a rubber sledgehammer. Harsh but effective!

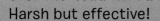

HABITAT

Although they are often found shuffling around Goosebump Manor, Dearly-Departed Nibblies are created in the abandoned castle on MishMash Mountain.

Ultra rare!

JIGGLES
THE FIDDLY TWIDDLESTICK

Personality:
- ☑ Excitable
- ☑ Misty-eyed
- ☑ Sociable

Video games are not really my thing, although I did play the odd game of Moshi Kong in my youth. But ask a Fiddly TwiddleStick its favourite game and it will bore you silly with tales of the good old days when basic, blippity-blop video games were all the rage. Maybe that's why these sentimental Moshlings are always asking monsters to grapple with their clunky joysticks and pummel their buttons for old times' sake. All I know is that they make great stress relievers. Indeed, wiggling a TwiddleStick after a tough day is goopendously relaxing, although it gives you terrible blisters.

GAME OVER!

HABITAT

Vidiot Valley but you sometimes see Fiddly TwiddleSticks in the Games Starcade on Sludge Street.

LIKES New high scores and teak veneer

DISLIKES Sticky fingers and greasy blister cream

Ultra rare!

JIGGY
THE BAFFLED BIT

TO CATCH JIGGY:
COMBO UNKNOWN
TOP SECRET

Do you like puzzles? Me too! That's why I always pack a couple of Baffled Bits in my rucksack. But it's not because I want to start making jigsaws round the campfire. It's because I'm hoping to find more Baffled Bits! I believe these odd little Moshlings were once part of an enormous Puzzle Palace jigsaw. The trouble is they don't know where their other bits have disappeared to, so the second I turn my back they go looking for other Baffled Bits – and that's when I sneak after them! When they are not trying to piece together their lives, Baffled Bits enjoy scoffing Sudoku puzzles while studying geometry.

HABITAT

Originally they may have been part of a huge jigsaw in the grounds of Puzzle Palace. Nowadays they are scattered all over the world of Moshi.

LIKES Tweezers and biscuit tins

DISLIKES Doilies and shaggy carpets

UNCOMMON

KING TOOT
THE FUNKY PHARAOH

Personality:
- ✓ Jazzy
- ✓ Ancient
- ✓ Cool

TO CATCH KING TOOT:
COMBO UNKNOWN
TOP SECRET

I'm forever telling off my Moshlingology students for confusing Funky Pharaohs with Swingin' Sphinxes. But, as I keep explaining, Funky Pharaohs are the Moshlings who love tootling away on their solid gold saxophones. Unfortunately they are terrible musicians. But keep that to yourself or you might get turned into a sandcastle. How? It's easy thanks to that spell-spitting cobra headband. And I should know because I once ended up being shovelled into a Pretty Pyramid's bucket after telling a Funky Pharaoh to put a sock in it. Worse still, a Musky Husky had just used me as a sandy loo.

PARP!

HABITAT

Funky Pharaohs can usually be found tooting on the Yakkety Sax Sandbar near the banks of the River Smile.

 LIKES Cold, dark tombs and freeform jazz

 DISLIKES Mosquitos and bandages

COMMON

LINTON
THE MOLLYCODDLED MANAMANA

Personality:
- ✓ Pampered
- ✓ Nervous
- ✓ Particular

LIKES

Gooberry-flavoured milk and mini cookies

DISLIKES

Short sleeves and visiting the doctor

TO CATCH LINTON:

CRAZY DAISY — ANY + CRAZY DAISY — PURPLE + CRAZY DAISY — PURPLE

As well as being terribly fussy, Mollycoddled Manamanas are timid critters that rarely leave the cosy rock caverns they call home. Never seen without their trademark oversized jumpers (knitted by their adoring mummies), these wide-eyed Moshlings enjoy tinkering with toy trains, stamp collecting and brass rubbing. You might be wondering why an adventurous Moshlingologist such as myself would find these stay-at-home critters so fascinating? Well here's the thing: when I'm not swashbuckling my way around the world of Moshi, I like nothing more than sitting down and watching fresh paint dry whilst organizing my collection of toenail clippings. Hey, it's a hobby!

HABITAT

In the rockpools of Spoddy Sands but you might see the odd Mollycoddled Manamana looking for its mummy on Main Street.

RARE

LONG BEARD
THE VALIANT VIKING

Personality:
- ☑ Grumpy
- ☑ Stubborn
- ☑ Brave

TO CATCH LONG BEARD:

HOT SILLY PEPPERS · RED + HOT SILLY PEPPERS · RED + DRAGON FRUIT · ANY

I've heard a few tall tales over the years, especially whenever I've visited the Fibba Fjords. If you ever meet a Valiant Viking, prepare for suspect sagas of battle, bravery and broken helmet horns because these ocean-going Moshlings just can't stop babbling on about their dubious exploits. Fancy that! When they are not pillaging pickled goods or blowing up hot-water bottles, these beardy old fogies love play-acting with their rubber hammers – great fun until you're on the receiving end of their signature move, the Rubber Hammer Bammer! **OUCH!**

LIKES Pickled herrings and heavy metal

DISLIKES Hot-water bottles and chill-out music

HABITAT

Originally from the Fibba Fjords, Valiant Vikings still enjoy sailing the Seventy Seas aboard their longboats. Or so they say!

RARE

LUMMOX
THE HUMONGOUS HOGSNORTER

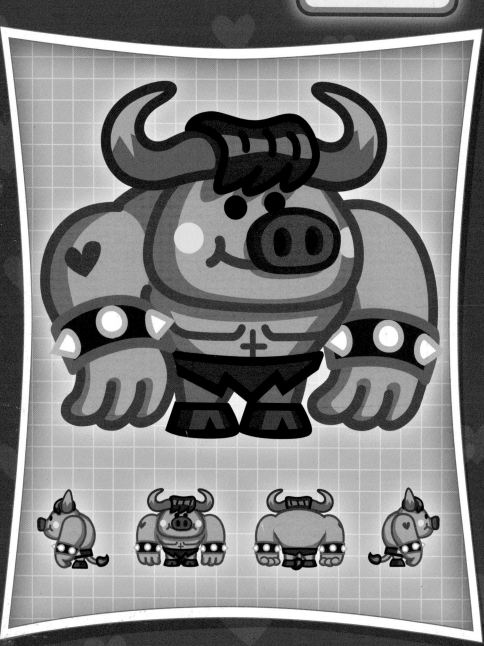

TO CATCH LUMMOX:

MOON ORCHID + MAGIC BEANS + LOVE BERRIES

Ooh, check out the biceps! And the abs! And the pecs! In fact Humongous Hogsnorters are buff all over because they spend hours pumping iron (well, OK, lifting little tins of gloop soup). I once challenged a Hogsnorter to an arm-wrestle and spent the next four weeks in Moshpital with a fractured paw. Raw strength aside, there's more to these buff beefcakes than muscles, as they enjoy knitting titchy loincloths whilst listening to retro hair metal. In fact I'm wearing the loincloth that was given to me as a get-well gift by the Hogsnorter who broke my paw at this very moment!

HABITAT

Head over to the gym near Bleurgh Beach and you might see a few Humongous Hogsnorters sunning themselves and striking poses.

LIKES

Bad action movies and Oochie Poochies

DISLIKES

Facefuls of sand and lazy Moshlings

UNCOMMON

89

LURGEE
THE SNIFFLY SPLURGEE

Personality:
- ☑ Germy
- ☑ Dim
- ☑ Sickly

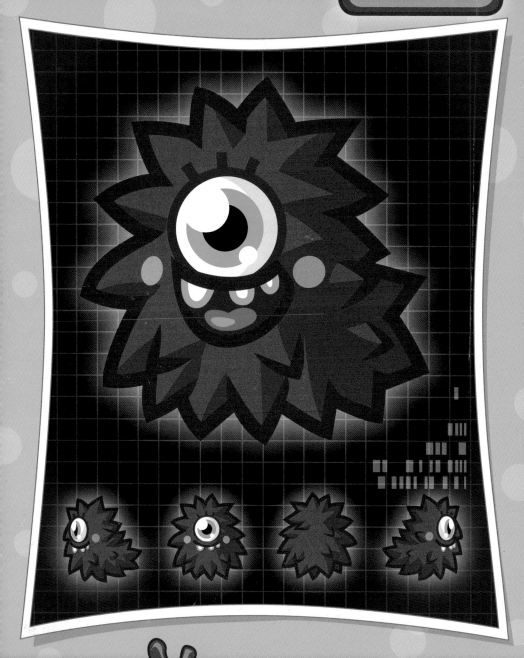

TO CATCH LURGEE:

DRAGON FRUIT	+	MOON ORCHID	+	CRAZY DAISY
BLUE		PURPLE		PURPLE

Please wash your hands because Sniffly Splurgees are highly infectious – in a good way, because despite the constant coughs and sniffles these bacteria-loving Moshlings soak up germs and viruses, keeping the world of Moshi bug-free. I discovered my first Sniffly Splurgee whilst looking for legless crabadoodles on Spewport Beach and I haven't caught a cold since. I even take a couple of Splurgees on my travels to help avoid catching any nasty bugs – and I'm not talking about gutterflies and ten metre skeeters. The only downside to owning a Sniffly Splurgee is that they stink of cough syrup.

WHIFFY!

HABITAT

Lurking in the Municipal Used Tissue Dump just outside Spewport Beach.

LIKES Eating tissues and collecting new viruses

DISLIKES Cold flannels and hand sanitizer

UNCOMMON

MARCEL
LE UPPITY CROC MONSIEUR

Personality:
- ☑ Bored
- ☑ Rude
- ☑ Superior

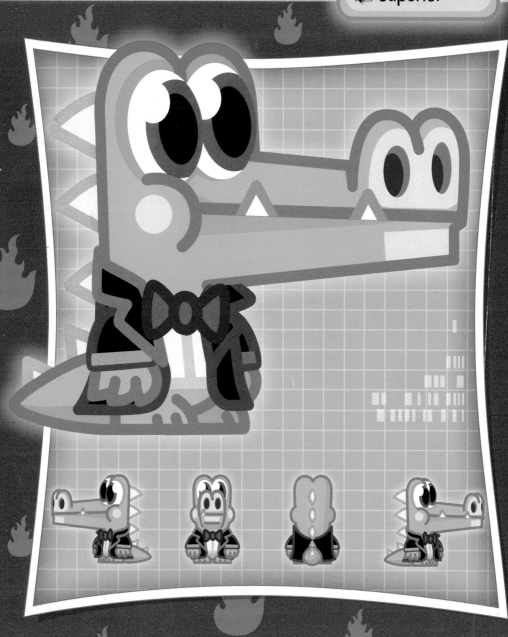

TO CATCH MARCEL: Complete CHOCODILE BLUES, SEASON 3, MISSION 2.

I'm not a big fan of bad service, and I believe the customer is always right, even if his whiskers are a bit straggly and he doesn't speak Uppity-ese. But for some reason these snippy-snappy Moshlings aim to displease. They really are phenomenally rude. And that's strange because most Uppity Croc Monsieurs work as waiters and butlers around the world of Moshi. So if you find a gutterfly in your soup, keep it to yourself or prepare for an Uppity telling off. It happened to me and I'm sure the Uppity Croc Monsieur who served me put a nasty surprise in my dessert. Or maybe it was supposed to taste of rotting barfmallows?

Ooh la la!

 LIKES Ham and cheese

DISLIKES Roast beast and bad tippers

HABITAT

Walk around the sidewalk cafes of Hoheehoh Boulevard and you're sure to see a few Uppity Croc Monsieurs.

RARE

MARSHA
THE BOGGY SWAMPLING

Personality:
- ☑ Hammy
- ☑ Slippery
- ☑ Friendly

LIKES
Swamp soup and B-movies

DISLIKES
Fishing hooks and gammy rays

TO CATCH MARSHA:
Head to Goosebump Manor and blast the ghosts in **HOUSE 2**.

Legend has it that the murky Slack Lagoon is contaminated with radioactive gloop. And I, for one, believe it because the last time I went diving there my fur went green and my gooberries started to glow. If you're wondering why I took gooberries with me it's because I was trying to attract Boggy Swamplings. I failed on that occasion but only because my gooberries were too fresh. You see these slime-guzzling Moshlings are attracted to rotten fruit and dead gutterflies. With their head-mounted fins, flappy-flippers and big buggy-eyes, Boggy Swamplings are a little scary and sometimes smell a bit like sulphur. But don't let that put you off. Oh OK, do!

HABITAT

The Slack Lagoon, but there have been countless Boggy Swampling sightings in the Neverglades.

Ultra rare!

MARTY
THE MOUTHY MOGUL

Personality:
- ☑ Melodramatic
- ☑ Brash
- ☑ Visionary

LIKES Yelling 'CUT!' and screaming at Flat-Tailed Fuzzles

DISLIKES All-Seeing Moment Munchers and ham

Feared by actors but loved by movie fans, Mouthy Moguls are the noisy Moshlings who think life is one gigantic movie set. Cover your ears if you see one in the street because it might throw a tantrum and yell 'CUT!', especially if it thinks you are acting in a wooden manner. You could write down what I know about movie-making on the back of a jelly bean, which is probably why I got into an argument with a Mouthy Mogul when I asked it to direct my documentary about Woolly Blue Hoodoos. Apparently I've got 'a face for radio' and 'the camera hates me'. Oh well, that's showbiz!

HABITAT

Most Mouthy Moguls live in lavish trailers parked in the back lot of the Moshi TV Studios.

TO CATCH MARTY:

Head to the Gombala Gombala Jungle and complete **MISSION 4**.

Ultra rare!

97

MICRO DAVE
THE POPTY-PING

Personality:
- ☑ Bright
- ☑ Smiley
- ☑ Wavy

TO CATCH MICRO DAVE:

HOT SILLY PEPPERS BLUE + HOT SILLY PEPPERS BLUE + STAR BLOSSOM PINK

What's cookin'? Why it's a Popty-Ping! These jolly Moshlings are the hottest critters in town but are forever being mistaken for Grinning Goggleboxes. Even experts such as myself get confused. I found a Popty-Ping wandering around the grounds of Bumblechops Manor a while back and spent ages trying to find its remote as I wanted to watch the latest Wobble-ade advert ('cos I'm in it). Oh well, at least Popty-Pings are friendly. Ask one to heat up some gloop soup or defrost your mutant sprouts and it will be glad to oblige. It might even give you a high five – but take care because those oven mitts get really hot. **PING!**

LIKES Baked potatoes and instant meals

DISLIKES Tinfoil and rubber chickens

HABITAT

Popty-Pings enjoy sitting on top of each other in the storerooms and warehouses of Stackem Anrackem Ridge.

Ultra rare!

MISTY
THE PLAYFUL PFFT PFFT

Personality:
- ☑ Spirited
- ☑ Inventive
- ☑ Cute

I can't abide graffiti so just imagine what I thought when I first visited CanCan Canyon. The whole place was covered in the stuff – and so was I the second I came face-to-face with a bunch of Playful Pfft Pffts. Yes, I realize spraying pretty patterns is a pleasant enough hobby, but Playful Pfft Pffts can't help puffing paint over everything in sight. 'Why say it if you can spray it?' was the first thing a Pfft Pfft said to me. These days, hip gooperstars such as Blingo use these canny characters to decorate their cribs with funky artwork. (Always shake before use.)

TO CATCH MISYY:

HOT SILLY PEPPERS — YELLOW + DRAGON FRUIT — PURPLE + SNAP APPLE — ANY

LIKES Being shaken up and big blank walls

DISLIKES Blocked nozzles and pins

HABITAT

CanCan Canyon but some Playful Pfft Pffts spray away from home near the Googenheim.

RARE

101

MRS. SNOODLE
THE SILLY SNUFFLER

Personality:
- ✓ Coy
- ✓ Innocent
- ✓ Powerful

TO CATCH MRS. SNOODLE:
Exclusive with **CARTE BLANCHE**
PLUSH AND *MOSHI MONSTERS*
***THE MOVIE* DVD**

She might be a Silly Snuffler but there's nothing daft about Mrs. Snoodle. The moment I hatched her (from the magnificent egg I discovered in a mysterious ancient temple) I knew she was a very special Moshling. And so did Mr. Snoodle – the little fella was instantly smitten! With her plume of rainbow hair, Mrs. Snoodle is easy to spot, so it's a good thing she's gone into hiding, as I'm certain Dr. Strangeglove would love to get his mitts on her. He's convinced she came from the Great Moshling Egg but I'm not so sure any more. I think I might have picked up the wrong egg.

OOPS!

LIKES
Mr. Snoodle and fluffy rainbows

DISLIKES
Microwavable Oobla Doobla and cameo roles

HABITAT

It's top secret but you can bet your fossilized fungus flakes Mr. Snoodle is doodling, canoodling and keeping Mrs. Snoodle safe. Needless to say, I've offered them a safe haven within my sanctuary.

Ultra rare!

MUMBO
THE PUNKY MONKEY

Personality:
- ☑ Anarchic
- ☑ Boisterous
- ☑ Nuts

TO CATCH MUMBO:
COMBO UNKNOWN
TOP SECRET

Never mind the beeswax, Punky Monkeys use custard to keep their crazy hairdos upright. But that's no surprise because these unruly Moshlings will do almost anything to stand out from the crowd, from scribbling naughty words on walls and swinging through the trees yelling tuneless protest songs to burping up banana skins. It's all rather silly if you ask me, although I must confess I once released a gang of Punky Monkeys into the Underground Disco just to see what would happen. Tyra Fangs nearly fainted and Roary Scrawl's eyes almost popped out. But Simon Growl said they were 'just what this competition was looking for' and signed them to HighPants Productions on the spot!

 LIKES Safety pins and churned butter

 DISLIKES Hippies and the system

HABITAT

You might see a Punky Monkey pogo-ing along Main Street, but these rebellious rockers originally come from Nyaargh Nyaargh Nook.

UNCOMMON

NANCY
THE FLOUNCY FANCY

Personality:
- ☑ Felicitous
- ☑ Flamboyant
- ☑ Gooey

TO CATCH NANCY:

DRAGON FRUIT — BLUE

+

STAR BLOSSOM — ANY

+

SNAP APPLE — ANY

Truth be told I don't know when my birthday is. It's a long story and only my long-lost Uncle Furbert knows the date for sure. But that doesn't seem to stop these sponge-based Moshlings singing 'Happy Birthday to yooou!' whenever I see them on my ranch. But it's not just me, they do it to every Moshi. In fact, Flouncy Fancies are always looking for something to celebrate, so it's a good thing their candles go out only when they are asleep. I once got stuck in a pothole with a Flouncy Fancy, and although its candles kept things nice and bright, I had to listen to it singing for what seemed like forever.

HABITAT

Flouncy Fancies stay fresh by shutting themselves in cake tins down on Cookie Crumb Canyon.

👍 **LIKES** Squashed tomatoes and stew

DISLIKES Bread and butter in the gutter

UNCOMMON

NUTMEG
THE WOODLAND WALNUT

Personality:
- ☑ Staunch
- ☑ Passionate
- ☑ Caring

TO CATCH NUTMEG:

HOT SILLY PEPPERS **ANY** + STAR BLOSSOM **YELLOW** + STAR BLOSSOM **ANY**

Just like me, these eco-friendly Moshlings are nutty about nature, and are always trying to protect the Moshi environment from interfering monsters. There have been many occasions when I've joined a few protesting Woodland Walnuts on marches down Main Street. I even painted myself orange for Save a Splatsuma Day and sat in a bathtub full of rotten gooberries to collect Rox for the new Bonkery Conkery Rescue Centre. When they are not hugging trees or whistling folk music to endangered naffodils, Woodland Walnuts enjoy shining their leafy ears with organic dewdrops.

LIKES Gardening shows and orienteering

DISLIKES Threshing machines and petrolheads

HABITAT

In the tall grass of Wingledeed Woods, but they often help out beneath the bio-domes of my Moshling Sanctuary.

UNCOMMON

PEEKABOO
THE OAKEY-DOKEY HOKEY-POKEY

Personality:
- ✔ Edgy
- ✔ Secretive
- ✔ Panicky

TO CATCH PEEKABOO:
Exclusive with
KATSUMA UNLEASHED.

The first time I spotted one of these shy critters I wasn't sure if it was a walking tree stump or a shy woodland critter in disguise. It's tricky to tell, even for an expert like me, because Oakey-Dokey Hokey-Pokies scurry away whenever you get near them. One thing is for sure, these highly-strung Moshlings will squirt slippy sap at anyone who tickles so much as a twig, so leaf 'em alone! I discovered this the sticky way when I got sapped in the eye whilst attempting to take a bark sample. Good thing I was wearing my protective Moshigoggles at the time.

SQUELCHY!

HABITAT

Usually in the Wobbly Woods but they have been known to shed their bark around the Unknown Zone.

LIKES

Check shirts and linseed oil

DISLIKES

Chainsaws and ramblers

UNCOMMON

PINESTEIN
THE JOYFUL JUICY BRAINIAC

Personality:
- ✓ Crackpottish
- ✓ Neurotic
- ✓ Kind

TO CATCH PINESTEIN:

MAGIC BEANS (YELLOW) + MAGIC BEANS (PURPLE) + LOVE BERRIES (PURPLE)

I thought I was pretty brainy until I bumped into a Joyful Juicy Braniac. With IQs of 256,948, these fruity critters can calculate the circumference of the Fun Park's big wheel in five seconds flat. But there's more to these science-loving Moshlings than mere mathematics because they also enjoy creating fruit zombies by re-animating slices of tinned fruit using giant potato batteries. I once snuck into the tunnels beneath the Moshi Fun Park and watched as a Joyful Juicy Braniac brought a pile of shrivelled splatsumas back to life. I'm still not sure how it was done but my fur was standing on end in terror!

LIKES
Algebra and laboratory conditions

DISLIKES
Low IQs and getting caught in the rain

HABITAT

In subterranean laboratories beneath the generator room of the Moshi Fun Park.

Ultra rare!

PIPSI
THE FIZZICAL PHEWBERRY

Personality:
- ✔ Obsessive
- ✔ Driven
- ✔ Energetic

All this wild adventuring across the world of Moshi takes its toll on my body. That's why I often turn to a Fizzical Phewberry when I need a good workout. Obsessed with keeping fit, these energetic Moshlings are always encouraging the citizens of Monstro City to stay active. Whether it's star jumps at breakfast time, push-ups in the park or touching toes at teatime, you can always count on a Phewberry to get your pulse racing. Ooh, it plays havoc with my gooberries but you know what they say, no pain, no gain!

TO CATCH PIPSI:

STAR BLOSSOM — RED + SNAP APPLE — RED + CRAZY DAISY — RED

HABITAT

You'll always find a few Fizzical Phewberries working out in Bubba's Gym but they are rumoured to come from Cardiofornia.

LIKES — Star jumps and exercise videos

DISLIKES — Sitting around and Oobla Doobla before bedtime

Ultra rare!

POSY
THE FORGETFUL FAIRY

Personality:
- ☑ Sweet
- ☑ Dreamy
- ☑ Mischievous

TO CATCH POSY:
COMBO UNKNOWN
TOP SECRET

If ever I spot a Forgetful Fairy fluttering around in circles I know it's probably trying to remember the way home. These cute little Moshlings can cast powerful spells, sprinkle fairy dust and even freeze time, but they are forever forgetting the simplest things, leaving the bath running and losing their keys. I can certainly relate to that, as I can be pretty forgetful myself. I once . . . er . . . um, oh bother, I forgot! Where was I? Oh yes, although they are absent-minded, Forgetful Fairies come in very handy around the home because they smell of raindrops and fresh flowers.

GORGEOUS!

LIKES Sewing daisy chains and brewing nectar

DISLIKES Fly swats and glockenspiels

HABITAT

Sparkle Nook near Copperfield Canyon but some Forgetful Fairies are attracted to beanstalk sap.

Ultra rare!

PRICKLES
THE TICKLY PICKLE

Personality:
- ☑ Prickly
- ☑ Tickly
- ☑ Loopy

TO CATCH PRICKLES:

HOT SILLY PEPPERS — RED
+
SNAP APPLE — RED
+
CRAZY DAISY — ANY

Look out, readers, it's Tickly Pickle time! And let me tell you, as well as being incredibly prickly, these potbound Moshlings are really, really tickly. The first time I touched one I felt as if thousands of sillipedes were crawling around my body. You see, every time Tickly Pickles sneeze they fire clouds of itching powder all over the place. I've only just got my safari suit back from the dry cleaners and it still feels itchier than a vest knitted from Elder Furi's beard trimmings. Talk about irritating!

HABITAT

Tickly Pickles enjoy chilling on windowsills but they often crop up in Itchypoo Park.

LIKES Rain and back scratchers

DISLIKES Sillipedes and wobbly saucers

RARE

PROF. HEFF
THE MOLECULAR CHEF

TO CATCH PROF. HEFF:
COMBO UNKNOWN
TOP SECRET

When it comes to cooking, I like simple things like mutant sprouts and gloop soup. Molecular Chefs, on the other paw, love over-complicating their cooking. In fact, they won't even poach a gooberry unless it's boiled under strict laboratory conditions. Then again, you haven't lived until you've tried their Slug Porridge with Vaporized Oobla Doobla. I first witnessed a Molecular Chef in action when I was judging a MonsterChef competition – the cheeky critter used one of my whiskers to decorate a dish of Nitro-charged Sludge Fudge. Needless to say, he won!

HABITAT

In research facilities just off Heston Highway near Gastro Gulch.

LIKES Foraging for fluffles and dissecting gooberries

DISLIKES Dirty surfaces and fast food

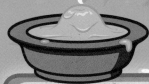

UNCOMMON

QUINCY
THE FRAIDY FUZZYFACE

TO CATCH QUINCY:
Complete **DAILY PRIZE QUESTS**.

I've had some bad luck in my time, but if you listen to a Fraidy FuzzyFace my misfortune pales into insignificance. These jittery Moshlings are always being frazzled by lightning, squished by falling pianos and attacked by swarms of sillipedes. Or so they say! It's hard to be sure because Fraidy FuzzyFaces rarely leave the house. And when they do they insist on wearing protective gloves, rubber boots and hard hats. I think they are great big scaredy cats, but I still do my best to avoid hanging out with them too much.

BEWARE: DANGER AHEAD!

CAUTION!

HABITAT

Fraidy FuzzyFaces live on Eek Street but I've spotted a few dashing along Ooh La Lane with their hands on their heads.

👍 **LIKES**

Staying in and reading the *Daily Fail*

👎 **DISLIKES**

Going out and toffee apples

RARE

RANDALL
THE LITTLE RED RIDING WOLF

Personality:
- ☑ Split
- ☑ Ravenous
- ☑ Charming

LIKES Comfy beds and granny-style nightcaps

DISLIKES Tuneless howling and half moons

TO CATCH RANDALL:
Head to Goosebump Manor and blast the ghosts in **HOUSE 3**.

My, what big fangs they have! But there's more to Little Red Riding Wolves than sharp teeth and wild eyes because these howling-mad Moshlings harbour a deep secret: they transform into sweet little girls whenever there's a full moon. Barking mad, eh! I once hid in a wardrobe in a cabin in Fabled Forest and watched in horror as a Little Red Riding Wolf transformed. It was hideous! For a start the wardrobe stank of mothballs and I couldn't breathe. Worse still, the moonstruck Moshling spotted me and chased me till dawn. I've still got a rip in the seat of my pants to prove it!

HABITAT

Little Red Riding Wolves enjoy skulking around log cabins but they are thought to come from the Fabled Forest.

RARE

RAFFLES
THE SNEAKY TEALEAF

TO CATCH RAFFLES:
Complete the
GOOGENHEIST MISSION,
SEASON 3, PART 3.

There have been several unexplained break-ins at Bumblechops Manor and I'm pretty sure a Sneaky TeaLeaf is to blame for most of them. Hide your valuables and lock up your socks because Sneaky TeaLeafs just can't resist pinching things. But don't worry, these reformed crooks always return their loot. They've even been known to sneak into houses and put things back where they found 'em, especially odd socks. They wipe away any paw prints with their bushy tails.

HABITAT

Sneaky TeaLeafs love scampering around rooftops, but you might find a few in Klepto Canyon where they enjoy sorting out stolen socks.

LIKES Modern art and open windows

DISLIKES Tripwires and the long arm of the law

Ultra rare!

127

SHIMMY
THE SELFISH SHELLFISH

Personality:
- ✓ Rash
- ✓ Petty
- ✓ Immature

TO CATCH SHIMMY:

MAGIC BEANS	LOVE BERRIES	CRAZY DAISY
ANY	ANY	ANY

'Sthelfish threllpish . . . thelfifth felthith . . .'
Well have you ever tried saying 'Selfish
Shellfish' really fast with a mouthful of soggy
sand? I'm having a go right now but it's only because one of
these silly Moshlings made me do it in exchange for some of
the magical rainbow pearls it burps up every now and then.
You see Selfish Shellfish just love making monsters do daft
things. I have no idea why they always seem to target me!
But who cares, the joke's on them because I've got the
biggest magical
pearl collection
this side of
Clamshell Cove!

 LIKES Valley
Mermaids
and lip balm

 DISLIKES Lemon pips
and bottom
feeders

HABITAT

**Clamshell Cove,
but I've also seen
these ocean-going
Moshlings hiding in
treasure chests.**

COMMON

SHONEY
THE AMAZIN' BLAZIN' RAISIN

TO CATCH SHONEY:

HOT SILLY PEPPERS — RED + MOON ORCHID — BLACK + MOON ORCHID — RED

Goodness gracious, great balls of fire? Not quite, because these fiery fruit-based critters are actually Moshlings. Notorious for accidentally setting things on fire as they whoosh through Monstro City at breakneck speeds, Amazin' Blazin' Raisins are thought to ignite and take flight whenever they hear the phrase 'shrivelled grapes'. I used to take a few of these hot-headed Moshlings on my expeditions. Well, you never know when you're going to run out of matches. Sadly, I woke up one morning to find

an Amazin' Blazin' Raisin had torched my entire base camp, including the clothes I'd hung out to dry. Twisted firestarter? You bet. Worst of all, I had to travel all the way home in my jimjams!

LIKES Ill-fitting running shorts and hot eggs

DISLIKES Buckets of sand and dingalinging alarms

HABITAT

Wumf Foundry near Sprite Heights.

Ultra rare!

131

SLURPY
THE LICKITY LIZARD

Personality:
- ✔ Potty
- ✔ Irrational
- ✔ Silly

TO CATCH SLURPY:
Head to the **BEANSTALK PART 3** and complete **LOLLY LANDING.**

I found out the hard way that you must never lick a Lickity Lizard. You see their delicious mint-flavoured skin contains magical slime that temporarily sends you crazy. I gave one a lick when I'd run out of toothpaste in Dingleweed Swamp and I'm told I spent the rest of the day dancing around with my underpants on my head whilst nose-whistling Zack Binspin songs. Very embarrassing! But all this doesn't seem to stop these swamp-dwelling Moshlings from licking themselves. Maybe that's why they are always pulling stupid faces, leaping around like loons and gargling playground songs with dirty dishwater.

LIKES Dancing on the ceiling and crawling up the walls

DISLIKES Mouthwash and houseflies

HABITAT

Lickity Lizards enjoy playing in the tall reeds of Dingleweed Swamp.

RARE

SPLATTER
THE ABSTRACT ARTISTE

Personality:
- ☑ Avant-garde
- ☑ Snobby
- ☑ Obsessive

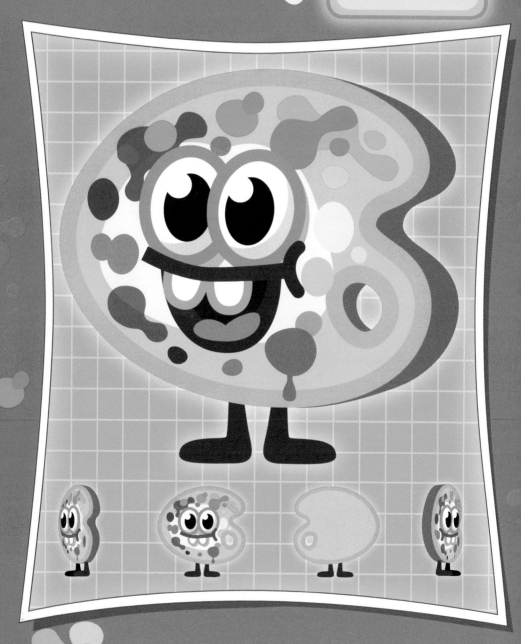

TO CATCH SPLATTER: COMBO UNKNOWN TOP SECRET

Is it art or an utter shambles? I really couldn't say. I don't go in for all this fancy modern art. But who cares about my opinion when an Abstract Artiste's sole ambition is to win the coveted Blurgh-ner Prize for Bafflingly Bonkers Art? That's why these crazy Moshlings spend all day flicking gluey glitter at passers-by and pickling slices of Oobla Doobla in huge tanks of fluorescent jelly. In fact, an

Abstract Artiste recently asked if it could construct a statue of yours truly (that's me!) made from freeze-dried mutant sprouts. No, thanks!

HABITAT

Go to Beret Boulevard and you're sure to find a few Abstract Artistes arguing about the merits of nose painting with marmalade.

LIKES Emptying bins over unmade beds and finger painting

DISLIKES Anything in the Googenheim and art critics

UNCOMMON

SPLUTNIK

 LIKES
Rocket fuel and space rock music

 DISLIKES
Bad special effects and trombones

TO CATCH SPLUTNIK:
Complete COSMIC COUNTDOWN, SEASON 2, MISSION 10.

Splutnik is the hyperactive Zoshling capable of rocketing from one side of the Silky Way to the other in less than twelve argh-secs. Apparently it's all down to his amazing jetpack. I wouldn't mind one myself to help rocket out of sticky situations. And just imagine how quickly I could round up Moshlings! Besides serving as chief engineer aboard the *Rhapsody 2*, this bubble-brained geek is a kazoo maestro, and also discovered the Bossanova Goopernova when he was still a space cadet. That would be even more impressive if I had the faintest idea what the Bossanova Goopernova is!

HABITAT

The planet Symphonia but Splutnik enjoys whooshing around the Way-Outta-Sphere strapped to his jetpack.

Ultra rare!

SPRINKLES
THE MAGICAL TINKLER

Personality:
- ✓ Joyful
- ✓ Playful
- ✓ Generous

TO CATCH SPRINKLES:
Complete GUSTBUSTERS MISSION, SEASON 3, PART 5.

Yes, they do look a bit like jolly watering cans but these big-nozzled Moshlings sprinkle more than just water. Tickle their tootsies and a rainbow shower of magical tinkles will cover everything within a three Moshimetre area, spreading joy and happiness. I often use Magical Tinklers to cheer up miserable Moshlings, and I even empty a few over my head on rainy days when I'm thinking about my long-lost Uncle Snufflepeeps. I should also mention that Magical Tinklers can toot tunes, which leads me to believe that they might be related to Silly Snufflers.

HABITAT

Magical Tinklers sometimes waddle around the gardens of Monstro City but are said to live somewhere over the rainbow.

LIKES Spreading joy and scoffing thumpkin seeds

DISLIKES Blocked nozzles and anyone called Alan

COMMON

SWEENEY BLOB
THE SPLODGY SUCKER

Personality:
- ☑ Gullible
- ☑ Yucky
- ☑ Nosy

TO CATCH SWEENEY BLOB:

HOT SILLY PEPPERS — ANY + DRAGON FRUIT — ANY + MOON ORCHID — ANY

My new Moshling Sanctuary is covered by enormous bio-domes, and Splodgy Suckers can't seem to get enough of them. You see, these gloopy critters love suctioning themselves to windows and listening in on the citizens of Monstro City. The only way to get rid of a Splodgy Sucker is to flush the loo. Why? Well, rumour has it they were once used as toilet plungers and hate that gurgly noise to this day. If the ones on my bio-domes start to block out the sunlight I just ask my pal Elder Furi to pull the chain that flushes his volcano. It scares them off in no time!

HABITAT

Glooped to windows but Splodgy Suckers also like hanging out under the pier at Breadcrumb Bay.

LIKES Eavesdropping and licking drainpipes

DISLIKES Toilet bowls and air freshener

COMMON

SWIZZLE
THE SWAGGERING SWINE

Personality:
- ☑ Precious
- ☑ Preposterous
- ☑ Boastful

TO CATCH SWIZZLE:
Complete **DAILY PRIZE QUESTS.**

Maybe it's their terrible eyesight but Swaggering Swines simply can't walk in a straight line. They usually swagger along the street in a ridiculous fashion, before stopping to 'tag' walls with graffiti using their rubbery, ink-soaked snouts. And don't be fooled by the blingy necklaces, they're actually great big pineapple rings, which I must confess are delicious!
I should know because I once caught a Swaggering Swine trying to write its name on the walls of Bumblechops Manor and it apologized by giving me its juicy bling. In fact that same Swaggering Swine now works for me, sealing my letters with its inky snout.

HABITAT

Head to Ker-Ching Canyon and you're sure to see a few of these trotter-tapping characters snorting along to the latest tunes.

 LIKES

Pineapple rings and loud snorting

 DISLIKES

Flashy Foxes and lampposts

RARE

TESSA
THE SHOOTING STAR

Personality:
- ☑ Radiant
- ☑ Enchanting
- ☑ Dreamy

TO CATCH TESSA:

MOON ORCHID YELLOW + SNAP APPLE ANY + SNAP APPLE ANY

Tamara Tesla believes they tumbled from space, but Elder Furi says they just pinged into existence. One thing's for sure, Shooting Stars are very special Moshlings because they can whoosh around faster than the speed of light, often arriving before they left. It's just a shame they communicate by twinkling and making swishy harp noises that only they understand. Many moons ago I attempted to translate this strange language as I thought it might be similar to ancient Custard-ese. Unfortunately it came out as gobbledegook and the only words I could make out were 'silly, look, that, monster, old' and 'at'.

HABITAT

Tamara Tesla thinks Shooting Stars are formed in slack holes beyond the Way-Outta-Sphere. That might be true but most of them live in and around the Twinkly-Dink Mines.

LIKES — Moon dust and goopernovas

DISLIKES — Space junk and being mistaken for Twistmas decorations

UNCOMMON

THREDDIE
THE THOCKITY WOCK

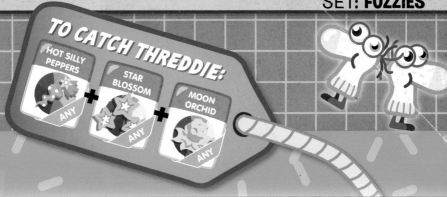

TO CATCH THREDDIE:

HOT SILLY PEPPERS — ANY + STAR BLOSSOM — ANY + MOON ORCHID — ANY

Geth what? Thockity Wockth can't thpeak pwoperly because they are always chewing fluff and yarn, especially when they are lonely. You see these 100% cotton Moshlings prefer travelling in pairs but are forever losing their fellow Thockity Wocks. That's why they often tie themselves together using the stray threads on their heads. I used to get Thockity Wocks to cover my golf clubs but they kept running away and getting lost. Nowadays I keep several at my Moshling Ranch but I often find them hiding in my sock drawer – and that's a problem as they bite.

OUCH!

LIKES Sweet feet and lint

DISLIKES Red underwear and tumble-dryers

HABITAT

Hiding in drawers or dangling on washing lines near Frayed Knot Farm.

COMMON

TOASTY
THE BUTTERY BREADHEAD

Personality:
- ☑ Reckless
- ☑ Friendly
- ☑ Energetic

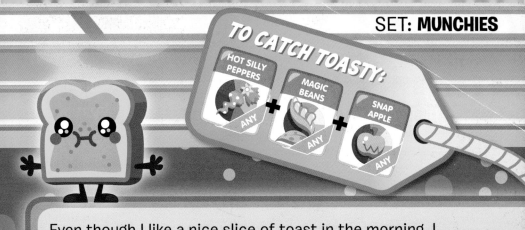

TO CATCH TOASTY:

HOT SILLY PEPPERS — ANY + MAGIC BEANS — ANY + SNAP APPLE — ANY

Even though I like a nice slice of toast in the morning, I wouldn't go so far as to say that Buttery Breadheads are the greatest things since sliced bread. No, no, no! For a start, these happy-go-lucky Moshlings enjoy spreading salty butter across their faces before leaping off tall buildings and trying to land butter-side up. And you should see the slippery mess they make when they don't succeed. I nearly broke my leg exploring Breadbin Estate. What's more, Buttery Breadheads hate the cold so don't be surprised if you catch one hiding in your toaster.

CRUMBS!

 LIKES

Runny eggs and four-slice toasters

DISLIKES

Being scraped and margarine

HABITAT

On top of each other on the Breadbin Estate, just outside Cookie Crumb Canyon. Buttery Breadheads brave enough to pop up in Monstro City are the toast of the town!

COMMON

TOOTS
THE BOOGIE-WOOGIE BUGLE

TO CATCH TOOTS:

MAGIC BEANS BLACK + MAGIC BEANS ANY + CRAZY DAISY ANY

In one ear, out the other? Totally, because Boogie-Woogie Bugles repeat everything they hear. But not with words, with little toots from their trumpety heads. Thankfully it's not too annoying because these ultra-hip Moshlings can parp into their hats, which act as jazzy mutes. I sometimes pop into the Purple Banana Jazz Club after a hard day's work for a few cheeky Bongo Coladas.

It's a great spot to observe Boogie-Woogie Bugles tooting away to each other. I can even parp a few notes of Bugle-ese using my great uncle's ear trumpet. **TOOT!**

LIKES — Satchels and brass polish

DISLIKES — Cigars and earbuds

HABITAT

Windypop Place, although you'll often catch Boogie-Woogie Bugles gigging in the Purple Banana Jazz Club.

UNCOMMON

TOPSY TURVY
THE TARDY TIMER

Personality:
- ✅ Unpunctual
- ✅ Worried
- ✅ Restless

TO CATCH TOPSY TURVY:

HOT SILLY PEPPERS — ANY + HOT SILLY PEPPERS — ANY + CRAZY DAISY — ANY

The first time I stumbled across Flippity Trip Farm I was amazed because the whole place was full of Tardy Timers, dashing about in all directions. You see, Tardy Timers are always running late. And that's most odd because the powdered egg that runs through their hourglass figures is rumoured to tickle their tummies whenever they are delayed. Then again, you'd be late if you spent all day doing handstands yelling, 'Ooh, it tickles!' Confused? You should be, because these crazy Moshlings are so manic they don't know whether they're coming or going.

Having said that, I still keep one in my kitchen to time my boiled eggs – and they're always far too runny!

HABITAT

Flippity Trip Farm, but you occasionally see Tardy Timers standing on their heads at train stations.

LIKES Runny eggs and hot feet

DISLIKES Digital watches and sand flies

COMMON

TUMBLES
THE NIFTY SHIFTY

Personality:
- ☑ Changeable
- ☑ Colourful
- ☑ Daring

TO CATCH TUMBLES:
Complete **DAILY PRIZE QUESTS.**

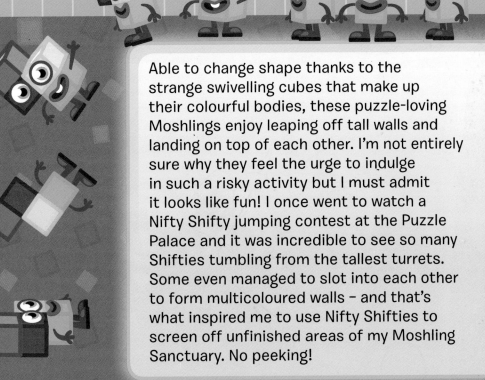

Able to change shape thanks to the strange swivelling cubes that make up their colourful bodies, these puzzle-loving Moshlings enjoy leaping off tall walls and landing on top of each other. I'm not entirely sure why they feel the urge to indulge in such a risky activity but I must admit it looks like fun! I once went to watch a Nifty Shifty jumping contest at the Puzzle Palace and it was incredible to see so many Shifties tumbling from the tallest turrets. Some even managed to slot into each other to form multicoloured walls – and that's what inspired me to use Nifty Shifties to screen off unfinished areas of my Moshling Sanctuary. No peeking!

HABITAT

Nifty Shifties live huddled together in Tumbledown Trench, an area just beyond the Puzzle Palace.

LIKES
Tumbling into space and balalaika music

DISLIKES
Apple pie and the law of universal gravitation

COMMON

TWADDLE
THE WADDLING FLOFFLE

Personality:
- ☑ Frivolous
- ☑ Sappy
- ☑ Soppy

TO CATCH TWADDLE:

Head to the **BEANSTALK, PART 1** and complete **BEANSTALK MISSION.**

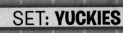

No, it's not a fat bat, it's a Waddling Floffle! Famed for their sap-slurping exploits, these beanstalk-bothering Moshlings will do anything for a sip of sap, especially if it's enchanted. Apparently it helps their titchy wings lift their tubby bodies off the ground. But not for long. Thump! I spotted my first Waddling Floffle when I was climbing a beanstalk near Lake Neon Soup. Since then I've heard rumours that there are thousands of these tubby critters near the top of the Great Moshi Beanstalk. How they got all the way up there is a mystery, but I'm determined to investigate just as soon as I find some Moshling porters brave enough to accompany me on the climb. Any takers?

LIKES
Enchanted sap and barbecued ladybird wings

DISLIKES
Greenfly and the rising cost of biscuits

HABITAT

You might see one fluttering around an enchanted beanstalk but most Waddling Floffles fall from the sky. Don't ask why!

Ultra rare!

UNCLE SCALLOPS
THE CRANKY CODFATHER

Personality:
- ✓ Tetchy
- ✓ Wise
- ✓ Regal

TO CATCH UNCLE SCALLOPS:

Complete **THE SECRET TREASURES OF POTION OCEAN MISSION, SEASON 3, MISSION 4.**

I've been searching for the legendary city of Splatlantis ever since I began studying Moshlingology, and I think Cranky Codfathers know more than they let on. Rumour has it that their ancestors once ruled the place. Sadly, these days they are better known for prodding passers-by with their plastic tridents and yelling rude comments.

Well, you'd be cranky too if you spent all day helping Moshlings across the road. Yep, that's right, these fishy fellas work as crossing guards on busy Haddock Highway. It's a perfectly good job but hardly a career fit for a king!

HABITAT

Cranky Codfathers can be found across the Seventy Seas but they sometimes pop into the Sea Mall to buy beard shampoo.

LIKES Mushy peas and wooden sporks

DISLIKES Ketchup and harpoons

RARE

VINNIE
THE GLAMSTER HAMSTER

Personality:
- ☑ Wild
- ☑ Vain
- ☑ Talented

TO CATCH VINNIE:

DRAGON FRUIT
ANY

+

DRAGON FRUIT
YELLOW

+

SNAP APPLE
ANY

The Boulevard of Broken Custard Creams is full of failed rock stars, particularly Glamster Hamsters. These hair-metal loving Moshlings just want to rock 'n' roll all night and party every day. When they're not playing air guitar or squeezing into spandex pants, these wild critters like screaming old Snotley Goo tunes while cruising along Main Street on customized trikes. Unfortunately, the music they enjoy is a bit out of fashion these days. Not that I'd know anything about that. The only time I grew my fur (aside from at Moshiversity) was when I was stranded in the Gombala Gombala Jungle without my scissors. How un-rock and roll!

HABITAT

The Boulevard of Broken Custard Creams, but they also hang out near the make-up counter in Horrods.

👍 **LIKES** Buns 'n' Toasties and hairspray

👎 **DISLIKES** Goo Fighters and brown candy

Roarshall

COMMON

WEENY
THE TEENY GENIE

Personality:
- ☑ Naughty
- ☑ Enchanted
- ☑ Funny

TO CATCH WEENY:
Head to **THE BEANSTALK**, **PART 4** and complete **CLOUD KINGDOM**.

The Caves of Shazam are truly fascinating but they are also where Teeny Genies hang out. Rubbing up one of these mischievous Moshlings the wrong way is definitely not to be recommended. I met one whilst searching for enchanted Rox and was told that my wish was his command – but only if I could moonwalk on my hands and pat my head at the same time. I gave it a go but was interrupted by sniggering. I looked up and realized that a whole bunch of Teeny Genies were floating above me, laughing their turbans off. Most embarrassing! Don't bother rubbing a Teeny Genie's lamp because all you will get is a face full of enchanted bubblegum!

 LIKES
Treasure and blowing bubblegum

 DISLIKES
Wonky Wizards and sesame crackers

HABITAT

Check out your loft, there could be a Teeny Genie hiding in an old bottle of Wobble-ade. Failing that, try the Caves of Shazam.

UNCOMMON

WILLOW
THE DAINTY DEER

Personality:
- ☑ Chilled
- ☑ Fragile
- ☑ Wary

TO CATCH WILLOW:

DRAGON FRUIT — PINK
MAGIC BEANS — YELLOW
SNAP APPLE — BLUE

Some Moshlings are so incredibly cute even I get tearful when I spot one in the wild. But the sight of a Dainty Deer scampering around in the snow, playing snowflake hoopla with its miraculous frozen antlers, trumps everything in terms of charm. Why, it's even enough to prompt the likes of Strangeglove to reach for his hanky, especially when you consider that life hasn't always been such fun for these lovable Moshlings. Believe it or not, they were once used to pull heavy, Rox-laden sledges from the Twinkly-Dink Mines.

AWWWW!

HABITAT

In the wintry wonderland around the foothills of Sillimanjaro, or in the windows of Horrods at Twistmastime.

LIKES Collecting snowflakes and figure skating

DISLIKES Red noses and white beards

Ultra rare!

WUZZLE
THE WANDERING WUMPLE

Personality:
- ☑ Wise
- ☑ Profound
- ☑ Wandering

TO CATCH WUZZLE:
COMBO UNKNOWN
TOP SECRET

There's no place like home, but try telling that to a Wandering Wumple. These ancient Moshlings have been roaming the world of Moshi looking for somewhere to settle ever since the Great Custard Flood of 99999.5. I've studied countless books in an attempt to locate their lost village but I fear it is probably buried under lashings of solidified custard. Besides, I think Wandering Wumples enjoy drifting around, as it gives them a chance to play with their magical heart-shaped charms that glow whenever a fellow Wumple is nearby. Well, at least they are never lonely!

LIKES Hokey quotes and upside-down meditation

DISLIKES Bustle and fast food

HABITAT

Here, there and everywhere.

RARE

YOLKA
THE BOILED BOFFIN

Personality:
- ☑ Intelligent
- ☑ Knowledgeable
- ☑ Logical

TO CATCH YOLKA:

DRAGON FRUIT ANY **+** **DRAGON FRUIT** ANY **+** **LOVE BERRIES** ANY

Here's a riddle for you: when is an egg not an egg? When it's a Boiled Boffin, of course! Brainy beyond belief, these eggheady Moshlings are renowned for their goopendous ability to remember anything, from the number of shoes worn by seventy splatterpillars to the exact time of my Great Uncle Furbert Snufflepeeps' disappearance – but only if they are wearing their magic spectacles. I often turn to the nearest Brainy Boffin when a little factoid has slipped my mind. I've even tried on a pair of those enchanted glasses, but they only seem to work if your head is shaped like an egg. No yolk!

 LIKES
Quizzes and pre-Custard Flood literature

 DISLIKES
Thinly sliced bread and Tardy Timers

HABITAT

Boiled Boffins live together in strange little egg cartons near Yellow Middle Meadow.

COMMON

YOYO
THE CREATIVE COYOTE

Personality:
- ✔ Hip
- ✔ Artistic
- ✔ Innovative

TO CATCH YOYO:
Complete **THE UNUSUAL SUSPECTS, SEASON 3, MISSION 1.**

Not to be confused with Hoxy Foxies, Creative Coyotes love making things, from yoghurt-pot rockets to sausage-skin legwarmers. When they're not busy starting new trends, these cool little Moshlings enjoy painting silly slogans on walls by dipping their bushy tails in paint. It's all rather avant-garde, and I must admit most Creative Coyotes' artistic efforts are far too trendy for an old-timer like me, although I did ask one to decorate the entrance hall of my Museum of Moshiness. Big mistake as it now looks like an explosion in a splatcurrant factory!

HABITAT

Usually found in Boreditch Fields, Creative Coyotes will hang out anywhere so long as it's heading east.

RARE

LIKES Recycled cardboard and fixed-wheel tandems

DISLIKES Cheap glue and beep-beeping birds

ZIGGY
THE QUIRKY KOALA

Personality:
- ☑ Rebellious
- ☑ Punky
- ☑ Talented

 LIKES Scoffing pukealyptus leaves and radical theatre

 DISLIKES Anything grey and shoe-staring

TO CATCH ZIGGY:

DRAGON FRUIT
ANY

+

DRAGON FRUIT
ANY

+

CRAZY DAISY
BLACK

Pump up the glam because Quirky Koalas are the music-loving Moshlings who enjoy face-painting and stomping around to rocking old tunes. I remember dancing with a pack of Quirky Koalas back in my Moshiversity days when I was still wearing platform boots and silvery eyeliner – hard to believe when you see me now but it's true. Thank goodness I threw away the photos. Oh yes, if you ever see a Quirky Koala sprinkling glitter on the ground, don't worry – it's probably preparing to mark its territory by performing a signature glitter angel.

HABITAT

Some say they fell from space but I believe Quirky Koalas hail from Stardust Street on Music Island.

UNCOMMON

ZONKERS
THE BONKERS WHIZZLING

Personality:
- ☑ Ridiculous
- ☑ Swift
- ☑ Giddy

TO CATCH ZONKERS:

HOT SILLY PEPPERS
ANY

+

STAR BLOSSOM
BLUE

+

MAGIC BEANS
ANY

You've probably seen pictures of the rocket-powered roller skates I use to keep up with fast-paced Moshlings. But even on eight wheels I'd struggle to snatch a Bonkers Whizzling. You see these out-of-control Moshlings adore whizzing around at breakneck speeds and sniffing out fun with their glee-seeking noses, which also act as brakes – ouch! Don't attempt to put your foot in a Bonkers Whizzling because the last monster to try ended up in Moshpital with tarmac up its nose. And I should know, 'cos it was me. Bonkers by name, bonkers by nature!

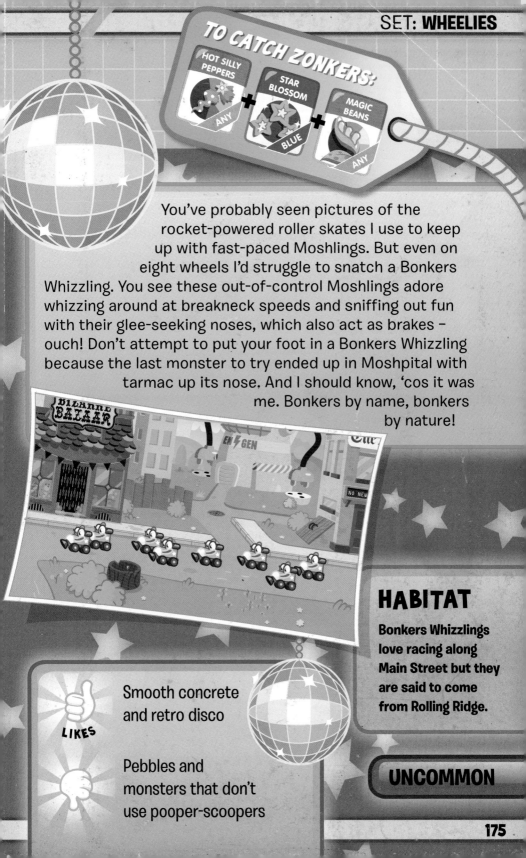

BIZARRE BAZAAR

EN GEN

HABITAT

Bonkers Whizzlings love racing along Main Street but they are said to come from Rolling Ridge.

👍 Smooth concrete and retro disco

LIKES

👎 Pebbles and monsters that don't use pooper-scoopers

UNCOMMON

FINAL WORD FROM
BUSTER

Well, there you have it, my fellow Moshling collectors.
I hope you enjoyed learning about all those wacky Moshlings.
Snuffy and I are packing for our next expedition right
now, so we'll keep you posted if we find any new species.
And if you come across any yourself, do feel free to get
in touch with me at Bumblechops Manor. Better still,
drop by for a cup of Mr. Tea.

And remember, as my Great Uncle
Snufflepeeps used to say,
you can never meet
too many Moshlings.

Ta-ta for now!